Encore

A Short Story Collection
edited by Peter Kneale & Owen Belling

PHOENIX
EDUCATION

Acknowledgements

"Nothing to be Afraid Of" and "William's Version" by Jan Mark, from
Nothing to Be Afraid Of by Jan Mark (Kestrel Books, 1980),
copyright © Jan Mark, 1980, by permission of Penguin Books.
"Teach Me to Dance" by Kerryn Goldsworthy, from her collection *North of the Midnight Sonata* (McPhee Gribble, 1989), by permission of Penguin Books
Australia Ltd.
"The New World" by William Lane, by permission of the author.
"High Tea" by Des Field, by permission of the author.
"Striker" by Matthew Fitt, by permission of the author.
"Mrs Cart" by Jack Cox, by permission of the author.
We have been unable to locate the copyright holders of the following stories,
and would appreciate any information that readers can supply:
"Tooking for a Lowel" by Patrick Campbell,
"Black Hole" by Geraldine Stowe and "Waking Up" by Kate Stephens

First published in 2003 by St Clair Press
This edition published by Phoenix Education Pty Ltd in 2004.
Reprinted 2005, 2006

Sydney
PO Box 3141, Putney 2112
Tel: (02) 9809 3579
Fax: (02) 9808 1430

Melbourne
PO Box 197, Albert Park 3206
Tel: (03) 9699 8377
Fax: (03) 9699 9242

Email: service@phoenixeduc.com
Website: www.phoenixeduc.com

ISBN 10 1 876580 71 2
ISBN 13 978 1 876580 71 1

Cover design by Sharon Carr, Graphic Divine.
Design and page makeup by Propaganda/goose.
Printed in Australia by Ligare Pty Ltd.

Contents

Introduction

Encore follows in the footsteps of *Exploring Short Stories Volumes 1 and 2* in providing a collection of short stories for use in the English classroom and is designed for Years 7-10 students. It is eclectic in nature, with texts ranging from classic masters of the form, such as Edgar Allan Poe, Guy de Maupassant and Katherine Mansfield, to modern exponents, such as acclaimed authors Jan Mark and Matthew Fitt and young Australian writers William Lane and Jack Cox. Amongst its pages you will discover humour, science fiction, fantasy, crime, romance and realism.

The stories are arranged according to a structure that may not be at first apparent. The collection moves through the subjects of the humour of life, fantasy and the world of the imagination, the relationship between past and present, the future, fear, crime and relationships. There is also a cyclical nature to the arrangement, beginning with the ironic 'The Capture of Walter Schnaffs' and finishing with a sequence of stories rich in irony. Indeed the central theme of this collection could be seen as "things are not always as they seem".

An audience calling for an encore is clamouring for more of the same. Paradoxically, as teachers we want our students to be calling for more because they see that English is not the same tired routine day after day. We want them to experience the English classroom as the place of the unexpected, a place where they can enjoy and explore the challenging world of meaning. We want them to be looking with anticipation for more.

The Capture of Walter Schnaffs

Guy de Maupassant

Ever since he entered France with the invading army Walter Schnaffs had considered himself the most unfortunate of men. He was large, had difficulty in walking, was short of breath and suffered frightfully with his feet, which were very flat and very fat. But he was a peaceful, benevolent man, not warlike or sanguinary, the father of four children whom he adored, and married to a little blonde whose little tendernesses, attentions and kisses he recalled with despair every evening. He liked to rise late and retire early, to eat good things in a leisurely manner and to drink beer in the saloon. He reflected, besides, that all that is sweet in existence vanishes with life, and he maintained in his heart a fearful hatred, instinctive as well as logical, for cannon, rifles, revolvers and swords, but especially for bayonets, feeling that he was unable to dodge this dangerous weapon rapidly enough to protect his big paunch.

And when night fell and he lay on the ground, wrapped in his cape beside his comrades who were snoring, he thought long and deeply about those he had left behind and of the dangers in his path. "If he were killed, what would become of the little ones? Who would provide for them and bring them up?" Just at present they were not rich, although he had borrowed when he left so as to leave them some money. And Walter Schnaffs wept when he thought of all this.

At the beginning of a battle his legs became so weak that he would have fallen if he had not reflected that the entire army would pass over his body. The whistling of the bullets gave him gooseflesh.

For months he had lived thus in terror and anguish.

His company was marching on Normandy, and one day he was sent to reconnoitre with a small detachment, simply to explore a portion of the territory and to return at once. All seemed quiet in the country; nothing indicated an armed resistance.

But as the Prussians were quietly descending into a little valley traversed by deep ravines, a sharp fusillade made them halt suddenly, killing twenty of their men, and a company of sharpshooters, suddenly emerging from a little wood as large as your hand, darted forward with bayonets at the end of their rifles.

Walter Schnaffs remained motionless at first, so surprised and bewildered that he did not even think of making his escape. Then he was seized with a wild desire to run away, but he remembered at once that he ran like a tortoise compared with those thin Frenchmen, who came bounding along like a lot of goats. Perceiving a large ditch full of brushwood covered with dead leaves about six paces in front of him, he sprang into it with both feet together, without stopping to think of its depth, just as one jumps from a bridge into the river.

He fell like an arrow through a thick layer of vines and thorny brambles that tore his face and hands, and landed heavily in a sitting posture on a bed of stones. Raising his eyes, he saw the sky through the hole he had made in falling through. This aperture might betray him, and he crawled along carefully on hands and knees at the bottom of this ditch beneath the covering of interlacing branches, going as fast as he could and getting away from the scene of the skirmish. Presently he stopped and sat down, crouched like a hare amid the tall dry grass.

He heard firing and cries and groans going on for some time. Then the noise of fighting grew fainter and ceased. All was quiet and silent.

Suddenly something stirred beside him. He was frightfully startled. It was a little bird which had perched on a branch and was moving the dead leaves. For almost an hour Walter Schnaffs' heart beat loud and rapidly.

Night fell, filling the ravine with its shadows. The soldier began to think. What was he to do? What was to become of him? Should he rejoin the army? But how? By what road? And he began over again the horrible life of anguish, of terror, of fatigue and suffering that he had led since the commencement of the war. No! He no longer had the courage! He would not have the energy necessary to endure long marches and to face the dangers to which one was exposed at every moment.

But what should he do? He could not stay in this ravine in concealment until the end of hostilities. No, indeed! If it were not for having to eat, this prospect would not have daunted him greatly. But he had to eat, to eat every day.

And here he was, alone, armed and in uniform, on the enemy's territory, far from those who would protect him. A shiver ran over him.

All at once he thought: "If I were only a prisoner!" And his heart quivered with a longing, an intense desire to be taken prisoner by the French. A prisoner, he would be saved, fed, housed, sheltered from bullets and swords, without any apprehension whatever, in a good, well-kept prison. A prisoner! What a dream!

His resolution was formed at once.

"I will constitute myself a prisoner."

He rose, determined to put this plan into execution without a moment's delay. But he stood motionless, suddenly a prey to disturbing reflections and fresh terrors.

Where would he make himself a prisoner and how? In what direction? And frightful pictures, pictures of death came into his mind.

He would run terrible danger in venturing alone through the country with his pointed helmet.

Supposing he should meet some peasants. These peasants, seeing a Prussian who had lost his way, an unprotected Prussian, would kill him as if he were a stray dog! They would murder him with their forks, their picks, their scythes and their shovels. They would make a stew of him, a pie, with the frenzy of exasperated, conquered enemies.

If he should meet the sharpshooters! These sharpshooters, madmen without law or discipline, would shoot him just for amusement to pass an hour; it would make them laugh to see his head. And he fancied he was already leaning against a wall in front of four rifles whose little black apertures seemed to be gazing at him.

Supposing he should meet the French army itself? The vanguard would take him for a scout, for some bold and sly trooper who had set off alone to reconnoitre, and they would fire at him. And he could already hear, in his imagination, the irregular shots of soldiers lying in the brush, while he himself, standing in the middle of the field, was sinking to the earth, riddled like a sieve with bullets which he felt piercing his flesh.

He sat down again in despair. His situation seemed hopeless.

It was quite a dark, black and silent night. He no longer budged, trembling at all the slight and unfamiliar sounds that occur at night. The sound of a rabbit crouching at the edge of his burrow almost made him run. The cry of an owl caused him positive anguish, giving him a nervous shock that pained like a wound. He opened his big eyes as wide as possible to try and see through the darkness, and he imagined every moment that he heard someone walking close beside him.

After interminable hours in which he suffered the tortures of the damned, he noticed through his leafy cover that the sky was becoming bright. He at once felt an intense relief. His limbs stretched out, suddenly relaxed, his heart quieted down, his eyes closed; he fell asleep.

When he awoke the sun appeared to be almost at the meridian. It must be noon. No sound disturbed the gloomy silence. Walter Schnaffs noticed that he was exceedingly hungry.

He yawned, his mouth watering at the thought of sausage, the good sausage the soldiers have, and he felt a gnawing at his stomach.

He rose from the ground, walked a few steps, found that his legs were weak and sat down to reflect. For two or three hours he again considered the pros and cons, changing his mind every moment, baffled, unhappy, torn by the most conflicting motives.

Finally he had an idea that seemed logical and practical. It was to watch for a villager passing by alone, unarmed and with no dangerous tools of his trade, and to run to him and give himself up, making him understand that he was surrendering.

He took off his helmet, the point of which might betray him, and put his head out of his hiding place with the utmost caution.

No solitary pedestrian could be perceived on the horizon. Yonder, to the right, smoke rose from the chimney of a little village, smoke from kitchen fires! And yonder, to the left, he saw at the end of an avenue of trees a large turreted château. He waited till evening, suffering frightfully from hunger, seeing nothing but flights of crows, hearing nothing but the silent expostulation of his empty stomach.

And darkness once more fell on him.

He stretched himself out in his retreat and slept a feverish sleep, haunted by nightmares, the sleep of a starving man.

Dawn again broke above his head and he began to make his observations. But the landscape was deserted as on the previous day, and a new fear came into Walter Schnaffs' mind – the fear of death by hunger! He pictured himself lying at full length on his back at the bottom of his hiding place, with his two eyes closed, and animals, little creatures of all kinds, approached and began to feed on his dead body, attacking it all over at once, gliding beneath his clothing to bite his cold flesh, and a big crow pecked out his eyes with its sharp beak.

He almost became crazy, thinking he was going to faint and would not be able to walk. And he was just preparing to rush off to the village, determined to dare anything, to brave everything, when he perceived three peasants walking to the field with their forks across their shoulders, and he dived back into his hiding place.

But as soon as it grew dark he slowly emerged from the ditch and started off, stooping and fearful, with beating heart, towards the distant château, preferring to go there rather than to the village, which seemed to him as formidable as a den of tigers.

The lower windows were brilliantly lighted. One of them was open and from it escaped a strong odour of roast meat, an odour which suddenly penetrated to the olfactories and to the stomach of Walter Schnaffs, tickling his nerves, making him breathe quickly, attracting him irresistibly and inspiring his heart with the boldness of desperation.

And abruptly, without reflection, he placed himself, helmet on head, in front of the window.

Eight servants were at dinner around a large table. But suddenly one of the maids sat there, her mouth agape, her eyes fixed and letting fall her glass. They all followed the direction of her gaze.

They saw the enemy!

Good God! The Prussians were attacking the château!

There was a shriek, only one shriek made up of eight shrieks uttered in eight different keys, a terrific screaming of terror, then a tumultuous rising from their seats, jostling, a scrimmage and wild rush to the door at the farther end. Chairs fell over, the men knocked the women down and walked over them. In two seconds the room was empty, deserted, and the table, covered with eatables, stood in front of Walter Schnaffs, lost in amazement and still standing at the window.

After some moments of hesitation he climbed in at the window and approached the table. His fierce hunger caused him to tremble as if he were in a fever, but fear still held him back, numbed him. He listened. The entire house seemed to shudder. Doors closed, quick steps ran along the floor above. The uneasy Prussian listened eagerly to these confused sounds. Then he heard dull sounds, as though bodies were falling to the ground at the foot of the walls, human beings jumping from the first floor.

Then all motion, all disturbance ceased, and the great château became as silent as the grave.

Walter Schnaffs sat down before a clean plate and began to eat. He took great mouthfuls, as if he feared he might be interrupted before he had swallowed enough. He shovelled the food into his mouth, open like a trap, with both hands, and chunks of food went into his stomach, swelling out his throat as it passed down. Now and then he stopped, almost ready to burst like a stopped-up pipe. Then he would take the cider jug and wash down his gullet as one washes out a clogged rain pipe.

He emptied all the plates, all the dishes and all the bottles. Then, intoxicated with drink and food, besotted, red in the face, shaken by hiccoughs, his mind clouded and his speech thick, he unbuttoned his uniform in order to breathe or he could not have taken a step. His eyes closed, his mind became torpid; he leaned his heavy forehead on his folded arms on the table and gradually lost all consciousness of things and events.

The last quarter of the moon above the trees in the park shed a faint light on the landscape. It was the chill hour that precedes the dawn.

Numerous silent shadows glided among the trees and occasionally a blade of steel gleamed in the shadow as a ray of moonlight struck it.

The quiet château stood there in dark outline. Only two windows were still lighted up on the ground floor.

Suddenly a voice thundered:

"Forward! Nom d'un nom! To the breach, my lads!"

And in an instant the doors, shutters and window panes fell in beneath a wave of men who rushed in, breaking, destroying everything, and took the house by storm. In a moment fifty soldiers, armed to the teeth, bounded into the kitchen, where Walter Schnaffs was peacefully sleeping, and placing to his breast fifty loaded rifles, they overturned him, rolled him on the floor, seized him and tied his head and feet together.

He gasped in amazement, too besotted to understand, perplexed, bruised and wild with fear.

Suddenly a big soldier, covered with gold lace, put his foot on his stomach, shouting:

"You are my prisoner. Surrender!"

The Prussian heard only the word "prisoner" and he sighed, "Ya, ya, ya."

He was raised from the floor, tied in a chair and examined with lively curiosity by his victors, who were blowing like whales. Several of them sat down, done up with excitement and fatigue.

He smiled, actually smiled, secure now that he was at last a prisoner.

Another officer came into the room and said:

"Colonel, the enemy has escaped; several seem to have been wounded. We are in possession."

The big officer, who was wiping his forehead, exclaimed: "Victory!"

And he wrote in a little business memorandum book which he took from his pocket:

"After a desperate encounter the Prussians were obliged to beat a retreat, carrying with them their dead and wounded, the number of whom is estimated at fifty men. Several were taken prisoner."

The young officer inquired:

"What steps shall I take, colonel?"

"We will retire in good order," replied the colonel, "to avoid having to return and make another attack with artillery and a larger force of men."

And he gave the command to set out.

The column drew up in line in the darkness beneath the walls of the château and filed out, a guard of six soldiers with revolvers in their hands surrounding Walter Schnaffs, who was firmly bound.

Scouts were sent ahead to reconnoitre. They advanced cautiously, halting from time to time.

At daybreak they arrived at the district of La Roche-Oysel, whose national guard had accomplished this feat of arms.

The uneasy and excited inhabitants were expecting them. When they saw the prisoner's helmet tremendous shouts arose. The women raised their arms in wonder, the old people wept. An old grandfather threw his crutch at the Prussian and struck the nose of one of their own defenders.

The colonel roared:

"See that the prisoner is secure!"

At length they reached the town hall. The prison was opened and Walter Schnaffs, freed from his bonds, cast into it. Two hundred armed men mounted guard outside the building.

Then, in spite of the indigestion that had been troubling him for some time, the Prussian, wild with joy, began to dance about, to dance frantically, throwing out his arms and legs and uttering wild shouts until he fell down exhausted beside the wall.

He was a prisoner – saved!

That was how the Château de Champignet was taken from the enemy after only six hours of occupation.

Colonel Ratier, a cloth merchant, who had led the assault at the head of a body of the national guard of La Roche-Oysel, was decorated with an order.

Tooking For A Lowel

Patrick Campbell

E ven now, after all I have been through, the thought of being unclothed in the presence of women has the power to make me half mad with anxiety. I drum my feet on the floor, perspire, and whistle loudly to drive the memory away.

So far, I, undressed, have come rushing at women twice. One of these occasions was connected with a shaving-brush.

I was lying in the bath one morning, when I remembered that I had left my new shaving-brush in my overcoat pocket. The overcoat was hanging in the hall.

Everything else was ready and in position. Shaving-mirror and soap; new razor-blade; toothbrush and paste; hairbrush, comb, and brilliantine tin; packet of ginger biscuits and a copy of *Forever Amber* on a chair beside the bath. When I wash I like to *wash*.

Everything was ready, then, except the new shaving-brush. I lay submerged for some time with just the nostrils and the whites of the eyes showing, trying to think of a substitute for a shaving-brush. Perhaps if the soap were rubbed on with the hand, and worked in? Or the toothbrush might be adapted to serve the purpose? The only difference between a toothbrush and a shaving-brush is that one is shorter and harder than the other, and the handle is fastened on in a different direction. But the toothbrush, properly employed, might be induced to work up a lather. I might even, by accident, invent a new kind of shaving-brush, with a long handle and a scrubbing motion....

All this time I knew I would have to get out of the bath and fetch the shaving-brush out of my overcoat pocket.

I got out of the bath, in the end, at a quarter past eleven. At that time I had a hairy kind of dressing-gown that set my teeth on edge if I put it on next to my skin. I ran out of the bathroom, roughly knotting a shirt about my waist.

In this flat the bathroom, bedroom, and sitting-room led off a passage. I ran lightly down the passage to the door, where my overcoat usually hangs. Then I remembered I had left the coat lying on a chair in the sitting-room. I ran more rapidly back along the passage, leaving footprints on the carpet. Already, I was becoming chilled and a little pimply. Passing the bathroom door I put on an extra burst of speed, and entered the sitting-room nearly all out.

It is difficult under such circumstances to make a precise estimate of the passage of time, but I think that a fifth of a second elapsed before I saw the charwoman standing by the window. She must have been dusting the bureau, but when she saw me she froze dead.

I, too, froze. Then I said "Waah!" and tried to leap out backwards through the door.

The charwoman very nearly got there first. The thought must have flashed through her mind that she would be better off outside in the passage, convenient to the main staircase, and so with a kind of loping run she came across the room.

We arrived upon the mat inside the door simultaneously. The mat went from under us, and we came down. I fell heavily on the feather duster which she was carrying, and the bamboo handle snapped. I thought my leg had gone.

We lay together on the mat for several moments, not shouting or anything, just trying to piece together in a blurry way exactly what had happened.

I came to my senses first. I was younger than she was, and probably more resilient.

I jumped up and made another break for the door. To my surprise I found it was shut, and not only shut but locked. I wrenched at the handle, conscious in the most alive way of my appearance from the back. The door was unyielding. I caught sight of a Spanish shawl draped across the top of the piano, and in a trice I was enveloped in it, an unexpectedly flamboyant figure.

Afterwards I remembered that the door opened outwards. I had gained the impression that it was locked by unthinkingly pulling it towards me.

And now the charwoman was also back on her feet. But to my horror I saw that she was taking off her housecoat – slowly and deliberately. It seemed to be her intention to disrobe. But why?

I watched her, wide-eyed. She folded the housecoat into a neat square. She placed it tidily in the centre of the table. "That," she said, "is me notice – and now me husband will have to be tole."

I fortunately never saw her again.

The other incident involving me and women took place when I was fourteen.

On this occasion I was again lying in the bath, but this time it was night, and I was reading *The Boy's Own Paper*. The rest of my family had gone out to the theatre, and I was alone in the house.

The particular edition of *The Boy's Own Paper* which I was reading must have contained a number of bumper tales, because when I came to the last page I found that the temperature of the bathwater had dropped from near-boiling to lukewarm. Checking back later I discovered that this had, in fact, been my longest sitting – ninety-seven minutes.

Taking care not to disturb the water, and set up cold currents, I reached out with one arm and dropped the *B.O.P.* over the side of the bath onto the floor. With the same hand I groped around in a gingerly fashion for the towel.

There was no towel. I had placed it on the chair, but now it had gone. I sat up in the bath, chilled, and peered over the edge, hoping to find it on the floor. There was no towel. I sank back into the water again, trying, as it were, to draw it round me.

There was no towel in the bathroom of any kind. And slowly I was freezing to death. I stretched out my right leg and turned on the hot water tap with my toe. Ice-cold water gushed out.

There was only one measure to be taken in this extreme emergency. I gathered my muscles, leaped out of the bath in a compact ball, wrapped the *B.O.P.* round me, wrenched open the bathroom door, and fled down the short passage leading to the linen cupboard. The linen cupboard door was open. I shot into it, and slammed the door behind me. Absolutely instantaneously I discovered that our parlourmaid, a young girl named Alice, was in the linen cupboard too.

What Alice and I did was to start screaming, steadily, into one another's faces. Alice, I think, believed that the Young Master had come for her at last.

In the end I got the door open again. It opened inwards, so that I was compelled to advance upon Alice in order to get round the edge of it. Alice, still screaming, welcomed this move with an attempt to climb the linen shelves and get out of the window.

I tried some word of explanation. What I said was: "It's all right, Alice; I'm tooking for a lowel." This had the effect of throwing her into a frenzy. She tried to put her head into a pillow-cover.

It was obvious that there was nothing more I could do, so I ran back into the bathroom, locked the door, and listened at the keyhole until I heard her run down the passage to the hall, sobbing.

The only other thing I would like to say is that now, whenever I have a bath, I make a list of the things I am going to need, and check it carefully before entering the water.

High Tea

Des Field

They loved to eat in the dark. It heightened their sense of taste and gave them a feeling of sharing a secret ritual. There was plenty on the table but, typical of a shared household, most had putrefied. Like the carton of milk. It stank to high heaven and neither Sheree nor Dave could bring themselves to go near it. There were limitations even in their world. The kitchen sink was stacked to the taps. Unwashed pots decorated with strings of dried pasta. Although Dave had investigated doing something about it he had decided to leave well alone, preferring to sit back and ruminate. It was what she liked about him. He was always thinking.

"You know we should get out," he said, tackling some left over pizza. "It's too dangerous now since that psychopath moved in."

Both noticed how jumpy they had been lately and even now, sharing a private moment, were still on edge. He was never far from their thoughts.

"I'm with you there," she replied, romantically sharing his slice. The cold cheese tasted like plastic but then, needs must . . . Recklessly she said, "Let's go tomorrow. Or tonight and –"

She didn't finish, as Barry appeared from nowhere. The weak moonlight picked out a leathery shine. "Go? Go where?" They didn't answer. Sheree lowered her head. They had been lovers once, but he'd never let her out of his sight. The habit was proving hard to kick. "You guys thinking of running out on me? Leave me here with this crap?" He took a mouthful of stale bread then slurped up flat beer that had spilled on the table. "Barry, you're gross. You make me sick." But Barry was enjoying making her squirm. He scratched his belly and scooped cream, at least three days old, from a nearby cake. It was almost walking off the table by itself. Pushing it into his mouth, he said, "Dave, you ain't got the guts to go. Besides, I'll have you for breakfast." Dave, who had been backing away slowly, stopped dead in his tracks. Embarrassed, he summoned the courage to speak. "I . . . I won't leave her here with you, you, you calculating bastard." Barry stopped chewing on a questionable piece of meat. "Yeah. You and whose regiment, you crumbling piece of shit." He moved closer as Dave and Sheree edged nervously around the edge of the table.

There was a sudden draft, which made them all move instinctively. But Barry didn't know what hit him as a rolled-up newspaper squashed him flat, the creamy contents of his stomach ejected halfway across the table. The other two cockroaches, seizing the moment, scuttled down the legs and across the floor, stopping only when they found safety under the fridge.

"It's that bloody psychopath, Sheree. We have to leave this place before we lose each other." She turned to him. "Well," she sighed with relief, "at least he's sorted our my relationship problem."

William's Version

Jan Mark

William and Granny were left to entertain each other for an hour while William's mother went to the clinic.

"Sing to me," said William.

"Granny's too old to sing," said Granny.

"I'll sing to you, then," said William. William only knew one song. He had forgotten the words and the tune, but he sang it several times, anyway.

"Shall we do something else now?" said Granny.

"Tell me a story," said William. "Tell me about the wolf."

"Red Riding Hood?"

"No, not *that* wolf; the other wolf."

"Peter and the wolf?" said Granny.

"Mummy's going to have a baby," said William.

"I know," said Granny.

William looked suspicious.

"How do you know?"

"Well ... she told me. And it shows, doesn't it?"

"The lady down the road had a baby. It looks like a pig," said William. He counted on his fingers. "Three babies looks like three pigs."

"Ah," said Granny. "Once upon a time there were three little pigs. Their names were – "

"They didn't have names," said William.

"Yes they did. The first pig was called – "

"Pigs don't have names."

"Some do. These pigs had names."

"No they didn't." William slid off Granny's lap and went to open the corner cupboard by the fireplace. Old magazines cascaded out as old magazines do when they have been flung into a cupboard and the door slammed shut. He rooted among them until he found a little book covered with brown paper, climbed into the cupboard, opened the book, closed it and climbed out again. "They didn't have names," he said.

"I didn't know you could read," said Granny, properly impressed.

"C – A – T, wheelbarrow," said William.

"Is that the book Mummy reads to you out of?"

"It's my book," said William.

"But it's the one Mummy reads?"

"If she says please," said William.

"Well, that's Mummy's story, then. My pigs have names."

"They're the wrong pigs." William was not open to negotiation. "I don't want them in this story."

"Can't we have different pigs this time?"

"No. They won't know what to do."

"Once upon a time,' said Granny, "there were three little pigs who lived with their mother."

"Their mother was dead," said William.

"Oh, I'm sure she wasn't," said Granny.

"She was dead. You make bacon out of dead pigs. She got eaten for breakfast and they threw the rind out for the birds."

"So the three little pigs had to find homes for themselves."

"No." William consulted his book. "They had to build little houses."

"I'm just coming to that."

"You said they had to *find* homes. They didn't *find* them."

"The first little pig walked along for a bit until he met a man with a load of hay."

"It was a lady."

"A lady with a load of hay?"

"NO ! It was a lady-pig. You said *he.*"

"I thought all the pigs were little boy-pigs," said Granny.

"It says lady-pig here," said William. "It says the lady-pig went for a walk and met a man with a load of hay."

"So the lady-pig," said Granny, "said to the man, 'May I have some of that hay to build a house?' and the man said, 'Yes.' Is that right?"

"Yes," said William. "You know that baby?"

"What baby?"

"The one Mummy's going to have. Will that baby have shoes on when it comes out?"

"I don't think so," said Granny.

"It will have cold feet," said William.

"Oh no," said Granny. "Mummy will wrap it up in a soft shawl, all snug."

"I don't *mind* if it has cold feet," William explained. "Go on about the lady-pig."

"So the little lady-pig took the hay and built a little house. Soon the wolf came along and the wolf said – "

"You didn't tell where the wolf lived."

"I don't know where the wolf lived."

"15 Tennyson Avenue, next to the bomb site," said William.

"I bet it doesn't say that in the book," said Granny, with spirit.

"Yes it does."

"Let me see, then."

William folded himself up with his back to Granny, and pushed the book up under his pullover.

"I don't think it says that in the book," said Granny.

"It's in ever-so-small words," said William.

"So the wolf said, 'Little pig, little pig, let me come in,' and the little pig answered, 'No.' So the wolf said, 'Then I'll huff and I'll puff and I'll blow your house down,' and he huffed and he puffed and he blew the house down, and the little pig ran away."

"He ate the little pig," said William.

"No, no," said Granny. "The little pig ran away."

"He ate the little pig. He ate her in a sandwich."

"All right, he ate the little pig in a sandwich. So the second little pig – "

"You didn't tell about the tricycle."

"What about the tricycle?"

"The wolf got on his tricycle and went to the bread shop to buy some bread. To make the sandwich," William explained, patiently.

"Oh well, the wolf got on his tricycle and went to the bread shop to buy some bread. And he went to the grocer's to buy some butter." This innovation did not go down well.

"He already had some butter in the cupboard," said William.

"So then the second little pig went for a walk and met a man with a load of wood, and the little pig said to the man, 'May I have some of that wood to build a house?' and the man said, 'Yes.'"

"He didn't say please."

"'Please may I have some of that wood to build a house?'"

"It was sticks."

"Sticks *are* wood."

William took out his book and turned the pages. "That's right," he said.

"Why don't you tell the story?" said Granny.

"I can't remember it," said William.

"You could read it out of your book."

"I've lost it," said William, clutching his pullover. "Look, do you know who this is?" He pulled a green angora scarf from under the sofa.

"No, who is it?" said Granny, glad of the diversion.

"This is Doctor Snake." He made the scarf wriggle across the carpet.

"Why is he a doctor?"

"Because he is all furry," said William. He wrapped the doctor round his neck and sat sucking the loose end. "Go on about the wolf."

"So the little pig built a house of sticks and along came the wolf – on his tricycle?"

"He came by bus. He didn't have any money for a ticket so he ate up the conductor."

"That wasn't very nice of him," said Granny.

"No," said William. "It wasn't *very* nice."

"And the wolf said, 'Little pig, little pig, let me come in,' and the little pig said, 'No,' and the wolf said, 'Then I'll huff and I'll puff and I'll blow your house down,' so he huffed and he puffed and he blew the house down. And then what did he do?" Granny asked, cautiously.

William was silent.

"Did he eat the second little pig?"

"Yes."

"How did he eat this little pig?" said Granny, prepared for more pig sandwiches or possibly pig on toast.

"With his mouth," said William.

"Now the third little pig went for a walk and met a man with a load of bricks. And the little pig said, '*Please* may I have some of those bricks to build a house?' and the man said, 'Yes.' So the little pig took the bricks and built a house."

"He built it on the bomb site."

"Next door to the wolf?" said Granny. "That was very silly of him."

"There wasn't anywhere else," said William. "All the roads were full up."

"The wolf didn't have to come by bus or tricycle this time, then, did he?" said Granny, grown cunning.

"Yes." William took out the book and peered in, secretively. "He was playing in the cemetery. He had to get another bus."

"And did he eat the conductor this time?"

"No. A nice man gave him some money, so he bought a ticket."

"I'm glad to hear it," said Granny.

"He ate the nice man," said William.

"So the wolf got off the bus and went up to the little pig's house, and he said, 'Little pig, little pig, let me come in,' and the little pig said, 'No,' and then the wolf said, 'I'll huff and I'll puff and I'll blow your house down,' and he huffed and he puffed and he huffed and he puffed but he couldn't blow the house down because it was made of bricks."

"He couldn't blow it down," said William, "because it was stuck to the ground."

"Well, anyway, the wolf got very cross then, and he climbed on the roof and shouted down the chimney, 'I'm coming to get you!' but the little pig just laughed and put a big saucepan of water on the fire."

"He put it on the gas stove."

"He put it on the *fire*," said Granny, speaking very rapidly, "and the wolf fell down the chimney and into the pan of water and was boiled and the little pig ate him for supper."

William threw himself full length on the carpet and screamed.

"He didn't! He didn't! He *didn't*! He didn't eat the wolf."

Granny picked him up, all stiff and kicking, and sat him on her lap.

"Did I get it wrong again, love? Don't cry. Tell me what really happened."

William wept, and wiped his nose on Doctor Snake.

"The little pig put the saucepan on the gas stove and the wolf got down the chimney and put the little pig in the saucepan and boiled him. He had him for tea, with chips," said William.

"Oh," said Granny. "I've got it all wrong, haven't I? Can I see the book, then I shall know, next time."

William took the book from under his pullover. Granny opened it and read, *First Aid for Beginners: a Practical Handbook.*

"I see," said Granny. "I don't think I can read this. I left my glasses at home. You tell Gran how it ends."

William turned to the last page which showed a prostrate man with his leg in a splint; *compound fracture of the femur.*

"Then the wolf washed up and got on his tricycle and went to see his Granny, and his Granny opened the door and said, 'Hello, William.'"

"I thought it was the wolf."

"It was. It was the wolf. His name was William Wolf," said William.

"What a nice story," said Granny. "You tell it much better than I do."

"I can see up your nose," said William. "It's all whiskery."

The Bottle Imp

Robert Louis Stevenson

There was a man of the Island of Hawaii, whom I shall call Keawe; for the truth is, he still lives, and his name must be kept secret; but the place of his birth was not far from Honaunau, where the bones of Keawe the Great lie hidden in a cave. This man was poor, brave, and active; he could read and write like a schoolmaster; he was a first-rate mariner besides, sailed for some time in the island steamers, and steered a whaleboat on the Hamakua coast. At length it came in Keawe's mind to have a sight of the great world and foreign cities, and he shipped on a vessel bound to San Francisco.

This is a fine town, with a fine harbour, and rich people uncountable; and, in particular, there is one hill which is covered with palaces. Upon this hill Keawe was one day taking a walk with his pocket full of money, viewing the great houses upon either hand with pleasure. "What fine houses these are!" he was thinking, "and how happy must those people be who dwell in them, and take no care for the morrow!" The thought was in his mind when he came abreast of a house that was smaller than some others, but all finished and beautiful like a toy; the steps of that house shone like silver, and the borders of the garden bloomed like garlands, and the windows were bright like diamonds; and Keawe stopped and wondered at the excellence of all he saw. So stopping, he was aware of a man that looked forth upon him through a window so clear that Keawe could see him as you see a fish in a pool upon the reef. The man was elderly, with a bald head and a black beard; and his face was heavy with sorrow, and he bitterly sighed. And the truth of it is, that as Keawe looked in upon the man, and the man looked out upon Keawe, each envied the other.

All of a sudden, the man smiled and nodded, and beckoned Keawe to enter, and met him at the door of the house.

"This is a fine house of mine," said the man, and bitterly sighed. "Would you not care to view the chambers?"

So he led Keawe all over it, from the cellar to the roof, and there was nothing there that was not perfect of its kind, and Keawe was astonished.

"Truly," said Keawe, "this is a beautiful house; if I lived in the like of it, I should be laughing all day long. How comes it, then, that you should be sighing?"

"There is no reason," said the man, "why you should not have a house in all points similar to this, and finer, if you wish. You have some money, I suppose?"

"I have fifty dollars," said Keawe; "but a house like this will cost more than fifty dollars."

The man made a computation. "I am sorry you have no more," said he, "for it may raise you trouble in the future; but it shall be yours at fifty dollars."

"The house?" asked Keawe.

"No, not the house," replied the man; "but the bottle. For, I must tell you, although I appear to you so rich and fortunate, all my fortune, and this house itself and its garden, came out of a bottle not much bigger than a pint. This is it."

And he opened a lockfast place, and took out a round-bellied bottle with a long neck; the glass of it was white like milk, with changing rainbow colours in the grain. Withinsides something obscurely moved, like a shadow and a fire.

"This is the bottle," said the man; and, when Keawe laughed, "You do not believe me?" he added. "Try, then, for yourself. See if you can break it."

So Keawe took the bottle up and dashed it on the floor till he was weary; but it jumped on the floor like a child's ball, and was not injured.

"This is a strange thing," said Keawe. "For by the touch of it, as well as by the look, the bottle should be of glass."

"Of glass it is," replied the man, sighing more heavily than ever; "but the glass of it was tempered in the flames of hell. An imp lives in it, and that is the shadow we behold there moving: or so I suppose. If any man buy this bottle the imp is at his command; all that he desires – love, fame, money, houses like this house, ay, or a city like this city – all are his at the word uttered. Napoleon had this bottle, and by it he grew to be the king of the world; but he sold it at the last, and fell. Captain Cook had this bottle, and by it he found his way to so many islands; but he, too, sold it, and was slain upon Hawaii. For, once it is sold, the power goes and the protection; and unless a man remain content with what he has, ill will befall him."

"And yet you talk of selling it yourself?" Keawe said.

"I have all I wish, and I am growing elderly," replied the man. "There is one thing the imp cannot do – he cannot prolong life; and, it would not be fair to conceal from you, there is a drawback to the bottle; for if a man die before he sells it, he must burn in hell forever."

"To be sure, that is a drawback and no mistake," cried Keawe. "I would not meddle with the thing. I can do without a house, thank God; but there is one thing I could not be doing with one particle, and that is to be damned."

"Dear me, you must not run away with things," returned the man. "All you have to do is to use the power of the imp in moderation, and then sell it to someone else, as I do to you, and finish your life in comfort."

"Well, I observe two things," said Keawe. "All the time you keep sighing like a maid in love, that is one; and, for the other, you sell this bottle very cheap."

"I have told you already why I sigh," said the man. "It is because I fear my health is breaking up; and, as you said yourself, to die and go to the devil is a pity for anyone. As for why I sell so cheap, I must explain to you there is a peculiarity about the bottle. Long ago, when the devil brought it first upon earth, it was extremely expensive, and was sold first of all to Prester John for many millions of dollars; but it cannot be sold at all, unless sold at a loss. If you sell it for as much as you paid for it, back it comes to you again like a homing pigeon. It follows that the price has kept falling in these centuries, and the bottle is now remarkably cheap. I bought it myself from one of my great neighbours on this hill, and the price I paid was only ninety dollars. I could sell this for as high as eighty-nine dollars and ninety-nine cents, but not a penny dearer, or back the thing must come to me. Now, about this there are two bothers. First, when you offer a bottle so singular for eighty odd dollars, people suppose you to be jesting. And second – but there is no hurry about that – and I need not go into it. Only remember it must be coined money that you sell it for."

"How am I to know that this is all true?" asked Keawe.

"Some of it you can try at once," replied the man. "Give me your fifty dollars, take the bottle, and wish your fifty dollars back into your pocket. If that does not happen, I pledge you my honour I will cry off the bargain and restore your money."

"You are not deceiving me?" said Keawe.

The man bound himself with a great oath.

"Well, I will risk that much," said Keawe, "for that can do no harm." And he paid over his money to the man, and the man handed him the bottle.

"Imp of the bottle," said Keawe, "I want my fifty dollars back." And sure enough he had scarce said the word before his pocket was as heavy as ever.

"To be sure this is a wonderful bottle," said Keawe.

"And now good morning to you, my fine fellow, and the devil go with you for me!" said the man.

"Hold on," said Keawe, "I don't want any more of this fun. Here, take your bottle back."

"You have bought it for less than I paid for it," replied the man, rubbing his hands. "It is yours now; and, for my part, I am only concerned to see the back of you." And with that he rang for his Chinese servant, and had Keawe shown out of the house.

Now, when Keawe was in the street, with the bottle under his arm, he began to think. "If all is true about this bottle, I may have made a losing bargain," thinks he. "But perhaps the man was only fooling me." The first thing he did was to count his money; the sum was exact – forty-nine dollars American money, and one Chile piece. That looks like the truth, said Keawe. "Now I will try another part."

The streets in that part of the city were as clean as a ship's decks, and though it was noon, there were no passengers. Keawe set the bottle in the gutter and walked away. Twice he looked back, and there was the milky, round-bellied bottle where he left it. A third time he looked back, and turned a corner; but he had scarce done so, when something knocked upon his elbow, and behold! It was the long neck sticking up; and as for the round belly, it was jammed into the pocket of his pilot-coat.

"And that looks like the truth," said Keawe.

The next thing he did was to buy a corkscrew in a shop, and go apart into a secret place in the fields. And there he tried to draw the cork, but as often as he put the screw in, out it came again, and the cork as whole as ever.

"This is some new sort of cork," said Keawe, and all at once he began. to shake and sweat, for he was afraid of that bottle.

On his way back to the port-side, he saw a shop where a man sold shells and clubs from the wild islands, old heathen deities, old coined money, pictures from China and Japan, and all manner of things that sailors bring in their sea-chests. And here he had an idea. So he went in and offered the bottle for a hundred dollars. The man of the shop laughed at him at the first, and offered him five; but, indeed, it was a curious bottle – such glass was never blown in any human glassworks, so prettily the colours shone under the milky white, and so strangely the shadow hovered in the midst; so, after he had disputed awhile after the manner of his kind, the shop-man gave Keawe sixty silver dollars for the thing, and set it on a shelf in the midst of his window.

"Now," said Keawe, "I have sold that for sixty which I bought for fifty – or, to say truth, a little less, because one of my dollars was from Chile. Now I shall know the truth upon another point."

So he went back on board his ship, and, when he opened his chest, there was the bottle, and had come more quickly than himself. Now Keawe had a mate on board whose name was Lopaka.

"What ails you?" said Lopaka, "that you stare in your chest?" They were alone in the ship's forecastle, and Keawe bound him to secrecy, and told all.

"This is a very strange affair," said Lopaka; "and I fear you will be in trouble about this bottle. But there is one point very clear – that you are sure of the trouble, and you had better have the profit in the bargain. Make up your mind what you want with it; give the order, and if it is done as you desire, I will buy the bottle myself; for I have an idea of my own to get a schooner, and go trading through the islands."

"That is not my idea," said Keawe; "but to have a beautiful house and garden on the Kona Coast, where I was born, the sun shining in at the door, flowers in the garden, glass in the windows, pictures on the walls, and toys and fine carpets on the tables, for all the world like the house I was in this day – only a storey higher, and with balconies all about like the King's palace; and to live there without care and make merry with my friends and relatives."

"Well," said Lopaka, "let us carry it back with us to Hawaii; and if all comes true, as you suppose, I will buy the bottle, as I said, and ask a schooner."

Upon that they were agreed, and it was not long before the ship returned to Honolulu, carrying Keawe and Lopaka, and the bottle. They were scarce come ashore when they met a friend upon the beach, who began at once to condole with Keawe.

"I do not know what I am to be condoled about," said Keawe.

"Is it possible you have not heard," said the friend, "your uncle – that good old man – is dead, and your cousin – that beautiful boy – was drowned at sea?"

Keawe was filled with sorrow, and, beginning to weep and to lament, he forgot about the bottle. But Lopaka was thinking to himself, and presently, when Keawe's grief was a little abated, "I have been thinking," said Lopaka. "Had not your uncle lands in Hawaii, in the district of Kau?"

"No," said Keawe, "not in Kau; they are on the mountain side – a little way south of Hookena."

"These lands will now be yours?" asked Lopaka.

"And so they will," says Keawe, and began again to lament for his relatives.

"No," said Lopaka, "do not lament at present. I have a thought in my mind. How if this should be the doing of the bottle? For here is the place ready for your house."

"If this be so," cried Keawe, "it is a very ill way to serve me by killing my relatives. But it may be, indeed; for it was in just such a station that I saw the house with my mind's eye."

"The house, however, is not yet built," said Lopaka.

"No, nor like to be!" said Keawe; "for though my uncle has some coffee and ava and bananas, it will not be more than will keep me in comfort; and the rest of that land is the black lava."

"Let us go to the lawyer," said Lopaka; "I have still this idea in my mind."

Now, when they came to the lawyer's, it appeared Keawe's uncle had grown monstrous rich in the last days, and there was a fund of money.

"And here is the money for the house!" cried Lopaka.

"If you are thinking of a new house," said the lawyer, "here is the card of a new architect, of whom they tell me great things."

"Better and better!" cried Lopaka. "Here is all made plain for us. Let us continue to obey orders."

So they went to the architect, and he had drawings of houses on his table.

"You want something out of the way," said the architect. "How do you like this?" and he handed a drawing to Keawe.

Now, when Keawe set eyes on the drawing, he cried out aloud, for it was the picture of his thought exactly drawn.

"I am in for this house," thought he. "Little as I like the way it comes to me, I am in for it now, and I may as well take the good along with the evil."

So he told the architect all that he wished, and how he would have that house furnished, and about the pictures on the wall and the knick-knacks on the tables; and he asked the man plainly for how much he would undertake the whole affair.

The architect put many questions, and took his pen and a computation; and when he had done he named the very sum that Keawe had inherited.

Lopaka and Keawe looked at one another and nodded.

"It is quite clear," thought Keawe, "that I am to have this house, whether or no. It comes from the devil, and I fear I will get little good by that; and of one thing I am sure, I will make no more wishes as long as I have this bottle. But with the house I am saddled, and I may as well take the good along with the evil."

So he made his terms with the architect, and they signed a paper; and Keawe and Lopaka took ship again and sailed to Australia; for it was concluded between them they should not interfere at all, but leave the architect and the bottle imp to build and to adorn that house at their own pleasure.

The voyage was a good voyage, only all the time Keawe was holding in his breath, for he had sworn he would utter no more wishes, and take no more favours from the devil. The time was up when they got back. The architect told them that the house was ready, and Keawe and Lopaka took a passage in the Hall, and went down Kona way to view the house, and see if all had been done fitly according to the thought that was in Keawe's mind.

Now, the house stood on the mountain side, visible to ships. Above, the forest ran up into the clouds of rain; below, the black lava fell in cliffs, where the kings of old lay buried. A garden bloomed about that house with every hue of flowers; and there was an orchard of papaia on the one hand and an orchard of breadfruit on the other, and right in front, toward the sea, a ship's mast had been rigged up and bore a flag. As for the house, it was three storeys high, with great chambers and broad balconies on each. The windows were of glass, so excellent that it was as clear as water and as bright as day. All manner of furniture adorned the chambers. Pictures hung upon the wall in golden frames: pictures of ships, and men fighting, and of the most beautiful women, and of singular places; nowhere in the world are there pictures of so bright a colour as those Keawe found hanging in his house. As for the knick-knacks, they were extraordinary fine; chiming clocks and musical boxes, little men with nodding heads, books filled with pictures, weapons of price from all quarters of the world, and the most elegant puzzles to entertain the leisure of a solitary man. And as no one would care to live in such chambers, only to walk through and view them, the balconies were made so broad that a whole town might have lived upon them in delight; and Keawe knew not which to prefer, whether the back porch, where you got the land breeze, and looked upon the orchards and the flowers, or the front balcony, where you could drink the wind of the sea, and look down the steep wall of the mountain and see the Hall going by once a week or so between Hookena and the hills of Pele, or the schooners plying up the coast for wood and ava and bananas.

When they had viewed all, Keawe and Lopaka sat on the porch.

"Well," asked Lopaka, "is it all as you designed?"

"Words cannot utter it," said Keawe. "It is better than I dreamed, and I am sick with satisfaction."

"There is but one thing to consider," said Lopaka; "all this may be quite natural, and the bottle imp have nothing whatever to say to it. If I were to buy the bottle, and got no schooner after all, I should have put my hand in the fire for nothing. I gave you my word, I know; but yet I think you would not grudge me one more proof."

"I have sworn I would take no more favours," said Keawe. "I have gone already deep enough."

"This is no favour I am thinking of," replied Lopaka. "It is only to see the imp himself. There is nothing to be gained by that, and so nothing to be ashamed of; and yet, if I once saw him, I should be sure of the whole matter. So indulge me so far, and let me see the imp; and, after that, here is the money in my hand, and I will buy it."

"There is only one thing I am afraid of," said Keawe. "The imp may be very ugly to view; and if you once set eyes upon him you might be very undesirous of the bottle."

"I am a man of my word," said Lopaka. "And here is the money betwixt us."

"Very well," replied Keawe. "I have a curiosity myself. So come, let us have one look at you, Mr Imp."

Now as soon as that was said, the imp looked out of the bottle, and in again, swift as a lizard; and there sat Keawe and Lopaka turned to stone. The night had quite come, before either found a thought to say or voice to say it with; and then Lopaka pushed the money over and took the bottle.

"I am a man of my word," said he, "and had need to be so, or I would not touch this bottle with my foot. Well, I shall get my schooner and a dollar or two for my pocket; and then I will be rid of this devil as fast as I can. For to tell you the plain truth, the look of him has cast me down."

"Lopaka," said Keawe, "do not you think any worse of me than you can help; I know it is night, and the roads bad, and the pass by the tombs an ill place to go by so late, but I declare since I have seen that little face, I cannot eat or sleep or pray till it is gone from me. I will give you a lantern, and a basket to put the bottle in, and any picture or fine thing in all my house that takes your fancy; – and be gone at once, and go sleep at Hookena with Nahinu."

"Keawe," said Lopaka, "many a man would take this ill; above all, when I am doing you a turn so friendly, as to keep my word and buy the bottle; and for that matter, the night and the dark, and the way by the tombs, must be all tenfold more dangerous to a man with such a sin upon his conscience, and such a bottle under his arm. But for my part, I am so extremely terrified myself, I have not the heart to blame you. Here I go then; and I pray God you may be happy in your house, and I fortunate with my schooner, and both get to heaven in the end in spite of the devil and his bottle."

So Lopaka went down the mountain; and Keawe stood in his front balcony, and listened to the clink of the horse's shoes, and watched the lantern go shining down the path, and along the cliff of caves where the old dead are buried; and all the time he trembled and clasped his hands, and prayed for his friend, and gave glory to God that he himself was escaped out of that trouble.

But the next day came very brightly, and that new house of his was so delightful to behold that he forgot his terrors. One day followed another, and Keawe dwelt there in perpetual joy. He had his place on the back porch; it was there he ate and lived, and read the stories in the Honolulu newspapers; but when anyone came by they would go in and view the chambers and the pictures. And the fame of the house went far and wide; it was called *Ka-Hale Nui* – the Great House – in all Kona; and sometimes the Bright House, for Keawe kept a Chinese man, who was all day dusting and furbishing; and the glass, and the gilt, and the fine stuffs, and the pictures, shone as bright as the morning. As for Keawe himself, he could not walk in the chambers without singing, his heart was so enlarged; and when ships sailed by upon the sea, he would fly his colours on the mast.

So time went by, until one day Keawe went upon a visit as far as Kailua to certain of his friends. There he was well feasted; and left as soon as he could the next morning, and rode hard, for he was impatient to behold his beautiful house; and, besides, the night then coming on was the night in which the dead of old days go abroad in the sides of Kona; and having already meddled with the devil, he was the more chary of meeting with the dead. A little beyond Honaunau, looking far ahead, he was aware of a woman bathing in the edge of the sea; and she seemed a well-grown girl, but he thought no more of it. Then he saw her white shift flutter as she put it on, and then her red holoku; and by the time he came abreast of her she was done with her toilet, and had come up from the sea, and stood by the track-side in her red holoku, and she was all freshened with the bath, and her eyes shone and were kind. Now Keawe no sooner beheld her than he drew rein.

"I thought I knew everyone in this country," said he. "How comes it that I do not know you?"

"I am Kokua, daughter of Kiano," said the girl, "and I have just returned from Oahu. Who are you?"

"I will tell you who I am in a little," said Keawe, dismounting from his horse, "but not now. For I have a thought in my mind, and if you knew who I was, you might have heard of me, and would not give me a true answer. But tell me, first of all, one thing: Are you married?"

At this Kokua laughed out aloud. "It is you who ask questions," she said. "Are you married yourself?"

"Indeed, Kokua, I am not," replied Keawe, "and never thought to be until this hour. But here is the plain truth. I have met you here at the roadside, and I saw your eyes, which are like the stars, and my heart went to you as swift as a bird. And so now, if you want none of me, say so, and I will go on to my own place; but if you think me no worse than any other young man, say so, too, and I will turn aside to your father's for the night, and tomorrow I will talk with the good man."

Kokua said never a word, but she looked at the sea and laughed.

"Kokua," said Keawe, "if you say nothing, I will take that for the good answer; so let us be stepping to your father's door."

She went on ahead of him, still without speech; only sometimes she glanced back and glanced away again, and she kept the strings of her hat in her mouth.

Now, when they had come to the door, Kiano came out on his verandah, and cried out and welcomed Keawe by name. At that the girl looked over, for the fame of the great house had come to her ears; and, to be sure, it was a great temptation. All that evening they were very merry together; and the girl was as bold as brass under the eyes of her parents, and made a mock of Keawe, for she had a quick wit. The next day he had a word with Kiano, and found the girl alone.

"Kokua," said he, "you made a mock of me all the evening; and it is still time to bid me go. I would not tell you who I was, because I have so fine a house, and I feared you would think too much of that house and too little of the man that loves you. Now you know all, and if you wish to have seen the last of me, say so at once."

"No," said Kokua; but this time she did not laugh, nor did Keawe ask for more.

This was the wooing of Keawe; things had gone quickly; but so an arrow goes, and the ball of a rifle swifter still, and yet both may strike the target. Things had gone fast, but they had gone far also, and the thought of Keawe rang in the maiden's head; she heard his voice in the breach of the surf upon the lava, and for this young man that she had seen but twice she would have left father and mother and her native islands. As for Keawe himself, his horse flew up the path of the mountain under the cliff of tombs, and the sound of the hoofs, and the sound of Keawe singing to himself for pleasure, echoed in the caverns of the dead. He came to the Bright House, and still he was singing. He sat and ate in the broad balcony, and the Chinese man wondered at his master, to hear how he sang between the mouthfuls. The sun went down into the sea, and the night came; and Keawe walked the balconies by lamplight, high on the mountains, and the voice of his singing startled men on ships.

"Here am I now upon my high place," he said to himself. "Life may be no better; this is the mountain top; and all shelves about me toward the worse. For the first time I will light up the chambers, and bathe in my fine bath with the hot water and the cold, and sleep alone in the bed of my bridal chamber."

So the Chinese man had word, and he must rise from sleep and light the furnaces; and as he wrought below, beside the boilers, he heard his master singing and rejoicing above him in the lighted chambers. When the water began to be hot the Chinese man cried to his master; and Keawe went into the bathroom; and the Chinese man heard him sing as he filled the marble basin; and heard him sing, and the singing broken, as he undressed; until of a sudden, the song ceased. The Chinese man listened, and listened; he called up the house to Keawe to ask if all were well, and Keawe answered him "Yes," and bade him go to bed; but there was no more singing in the Bright House; and all night long, the Chinese man heard his master's feet go round and round the balconies without repose.

Now the truth of it was this: as Keawe undressed for his bath, he spied upon his flesh a patch like a patch of lichen on a rock, and it was then that he stopped singing. For he knew the likeness of that patch, and knew that he was fallen in the Chinese Evil.

Now, it is a sad thing for any man to fall into this sickness. And it would be a sad thing for anyone to leave a house so beautiful and so commodious, and depart from all his friends to the north coast of Molokai between the mighty cliff and the sea breakers. But what was that to the case of the man Keawe, he who had met his love but yesterday, and won her but that morning, and now saw all his hopes break, in a moment, like a piece of glass?

Awhile he sat upon the edge of the bath; then sprang, with a cry, and ran outside; and to and fro, to and fro, along the balcony, like one despairing.

"Very willingly could I leave Hawaii, the home of my fathers," Keawe was thinking. "Very lightly could I leave my house, the high-placed, the many-windowed, here upon the mountains. Very bravely could I go to Molokai, to Kalaupapa by the cliffs, to live with the smitten and to sleep there, far from my fathers. But what wrong have I done, what sin lies upon my soul, that I should have encountered Kokua coming cool from the sea-water in the evening? Kokua, the soul ensnarer! Kokua, the light of my life! Her may I never wed, her may I look upon no longer, her may I no more handle with my loving hand; and it is for this, it is for you, O Kokua! that I pour my lamentations!"

Now you are to observe what sort of a man Keawe was, for he might have dwelt there in the Bright House for years, and no one been the wiser of his sickness; but he reckoned nothing of that, if he must lose Kokua. And again, he might have wed Kokua even as he was; and so many would have done, because they have the souls of pigs; but Keawe loved the maid manfully, and he would do her no hurt and bring her in no danger.

A little beyond the midst of the night, there came in his mind the recollection of that bottle. He went round to the back porch, and called to memory the day when the devil had looked forth; and at the thought ice ran in his veins.

"A dreadful thing is the bottle," thought Keawe, "and dreadful is the imp, and it is a dreadful thing to risk the flames of hell. But what other hope have I to cure my sickness or to wed Kokua? What!" he thought, "would I beard the devil once, only to get me a house, and not face him again to win Kokua?"

Thereupon he called to mind it was the next day the *Hall* went by on her return to Honolulu. "There must I go first," he thought, "and see Lopaka. For the best hope that I have now is to find that same bottle I was so pleased to be rid of."

Never a wink could he sleep; the food stuck in his throat; but he sent a letter to Kiano, and about the time when the steamer would be coming, rode down beside the cliff of the tombs. It rained; his horse went heavily; he looked up at the black mouths of the caves, and he envied the dead that slept there and were done with trouble; and called to mind how he had galloped by the day before, and was astonished. So he came down to Hookena, and there was all the country gathered for the steamer as usual. In the shed before the store they sat and jested and passed the news; but there was no matter of speech in Keawe's bosom, and he sat in their midst and looked without on the rain falling on the houses, and the surf beating among the rocks, and the sighs arose in his throat.

"Keawe of the Bright House is out of spirits," said one to another. Indeed, and so he was, and little wonder.

Then the *Hall* came, and the whaleboat carried him on board. The after-part of the ship was full of Haoles who had been to visit the volcano, as their custom is; and the midst was crowded with Kanakas, and the fore-part with wild bulls from Hilo and horses from Kaü; but Keawe sat apart from all in his sorrow, and watched for the house of Kiano. There it sat, low upon the shore in the black rocks, and shaded by the cocoa palms, and there by the door was a red holoku, no greater than a fly, and going to and fro with a fly's busyness. "Ah, queen of my heart," he cried, "I'll venture my dear soul to win you!"

Soon after, darkness fell, and the cabins were lit up, and the Haoles sat and played at the cards and drank whiskey as their custom is; but Keawe walked the deck all night; and all the next day, as they steamed under the lee of Maui or of Molokai, he was still pacing to and fro like a wild animal in a menagerie.

Towards evening they passed Diamond Head, and came to the pier of Honolulu. Keawe stepped out among the crowd and began to ask for Lopaka. It seemed he had become the owner of a schooner – none better in the islands – and was gone upon an adventure as far as Pola-Pola or Kahiki; so there was no help to be looked for from Lopaka. Keawe called to mind a friend of his, a lawyer in the town (I must not tell his name), and inquired of him. They said he was grown suddenly rich, and had a fine new house upon Waikiki shore; and this put a thought in Keawe's head, and he called a hack and drove to the lawyer's house.

The house was all brand new, and the trees in the garden no greater than walking-sticks, and the lawyer, when he came, had the air of a man well pleased.

"What can I do to serve you?" said the lawyer.

"You are a friend of Lopaka's," replied Keawe, "and Lopaka purchased from me a certain piece of goods that I thought you might enable me to trace."

The lawyer's face became very dark. "I do not profess to misunderstand you, Mr Keawe," said he, "though this is an ugly business to be stirring in. You may be sure I know nothing, but yet I have a guess, and if you would apply in a certain quarter I think you might have news."

And he named the name of a man, which, again, I had better not repeat. So it was for days, and Keawe went from one to another, finding everywhere new clothes and carriages, and fine new houses and men everywhere in great contentment, although, to be sure, when he hinted at his business their faces would cloud over.

"No doubt I am upon the track," thought Keawe. "These new clothes and carriages are all the gifts of the little imp, and these glad faces are the faces of men who have taken their profit and got rid of the accursed thing in safety. When I see pale cheeks and hear sighing, I shall know that I am near the bottle."

So it befell at last that he was recommended to a Haole in Beritania Street. When he came to the door, about the hour of the evening meal, there were the usual marks of the new house, and the young garden, and the electric light shining in the windows; but when the owner came, a shock of hope and fear ran through Keawe; for here was a young man, white as a corpse, and black about the eyes, the hair shedding from his head, and such a look in his countenance as a man may have when he is waiting for the gallows.

"Here it is, to be sure," thought Keawe, and so with this man he noways veiled his errand. "I am come to buy the bottle," said he.

At the word, the young Haole of Beritania Street reeled against the wall.

"The bottle!" he gasped. "To buy the bottle!" Then he seemed to choke, and seizing Keawe by the arm carried him into a room and poured out wine in two glasses.

"Here is my respects," said Keawe, who had been much about with Haoles in his time. "Yes," he added, "I am come to buy the bottle. What is the price by now?"

At that word the young man let his glass slip through his fingers, and looked upon Keawe like a ghost.

"The price," says he; "the price! You do not know the price?"

"It is for that I am asking you," returned Keawe. "But why are you so much concerned? Is there anything wrong about the price?"

"It has dropped a great deal in value since your time, Mr Keawe," said the young man, stammering.

"Well, well, I shall have the less to pay for it," says Keawe. "How much did it cost you?"

The young man was as white as a sheet. "Two cents," said he.

"What?" cried Keawe, "two cents? Why, then, you can only sell it for one. And he who buys it –" The words died upon Keawe's tongue; he who bought it could never sell it again, the bottle and the bottle imp must abide with him until he died, and when he died must carry him to the red end of hell.

The young man of Beritania Street fell upon his knees. "For God's sake buy it!" he cried. "You can have all my fortune in the bargain. I was mad when I bought it at that price. I had embezzled money at my store; I was lost else; I must have gone to jail."

"Poor creature," said Keawe, "you would risk your soul upon so desperate an adventure, and to avoid the proper punishment of your own disgrace; and you think I could hesitate with love in front of me. Give me the bottle, and the change which I make sure you have all ready. Here is a five-cent piece."

It was as Keawe supposed; the young man had the change ready in a drawer; the bottle changed hands, and Keawe's fingers were no sooner clasped upon the stalk than he had breathed his wish to be a clean man. And, sure enough, when he got home to his room, and stripped himself before a glass, his flesh was whole like an infant's. And here was the strange thing: he had no sooner seen this miracle, than his mind was changed within him, and he cared naught for the Chinese Evil, and little enough for Kokua; and had but the one thought, that here he was bound to the bottle imp for time and for eternity, and had no better hope but to be a cinder for ever in the flames of hell. Away ahead of him he saw them blaze with his mind's eye, and his soul shrank, and darkness fell upon the light.

When Keawe came to himself a little, he was aware it was the night when the band played at the hotel. Thither he went, because he feared to be alone; and there, among happy faces, walked to and fro, and heard the tunes go up and down, and saw Berger beat the measure, and all the while he heard the flames crackle, and saw the red fire burning in the bottomless pit. Of a sudden the band played Hiki-ao-ao; that was a song that he had sung with Kokua, and at the strain courage returned to him.

"It is done now," he thought, "and once more let me take the good along with the evil."

So it befell that he returned to Hawaii by the first steamer, and as soon as it could be managed he was wedded to Kokua, and carried her up the mountain side to the Bright House.

Now it was so with these two, that when they were together, Keawe's heart was stilled; but so soon as he was alone he fell into a brooding horror, and heard the flames crackle, and saw the red fire burn in the bottomless pit. The girl, indeed, had come to him wholly; her heart leapt in her side at sight of him, her hand clung to his; and she was so fashioned from the hair upon her head to the nails upon her toes that none could see her without joy. She was pleasant in her nature. She had the good word always. Full of song she was, and went to and fro in the Bright House, the brightest thing in its three storeys, carolling like the birds. And Keawe beheld and heard her with delight, and then must shrink upon one side, and weep and groan to think upon the price that he had paid for her; and then he must dry his eyes, and wash his face, and go and sit with her on the broad balconies, joining in her songs, and, with a sick spirit, answering her smiles.

There came a day when her feet began to be heavy and her songs more rare; and now it was not Keawe only that would weep apart, but each would sunder from the other and sit in opposite balconies with the whole width of the Bright House betwixt. Keawe was so sunk in his despair, he scarce observed the change, and was only glad he had more hours to sit alone and brood upon his destiny, and was not so frequently condemned to pull a smiling face on a sick heart. But one day, coming softly through the house, he heard the sound of a child sobbing, and there was Kokua rolling her face upon the balcony floor, and weeping like the lost.

"You do well to weep in this house, Kokua," he said. "And yet I would give the head off my body that you (at least) might have been happy."

"Happy!" she cried. "Keawe, when you lived alone in your Bright House, you were the word of the island for a happy man; laughter and song were in your mouth, and your face was as bright as the sunrise. Then you wedded poor Kokua; and the good God knows what is amiss in her – but from that day you have not smiled. Oh!" she cried, "what ails me? I thought I was pretty, and I knew I loved him. What ails me that I throw this cloud upon my husband?"

"Poor Kokua," said Keawe. He sat down by her side, and sought to take her hand; but that she plucked away. "Poor Kokua," he said, again. "My poor child – my pretty. And I had thought all this while to spare you! Well, you shall know all. Then, at least, you will pity poor Keawe; then you will understand how much he loved you in the past – that he dared hell for your possession – and how much he loves you still (the poor condemned one), that he can yet call up a smile when he beholds you."

With that, he told her all, even from the beginning.

"You have done this for me?" she cried. "Ah, well, then what do I care!" – and she clasped and wept upon him.

"Ah, child!" said Keawe, "and yet, when I consider of the fire of hell, I care a good deal!"

"Never tell me," said she; "no man can be lost because he loved Kokua, and no other fault. I tell you, Keawe, I shall save you with these hands, or perish in your company. What! you loved me, and gave your soul, and you think I will not die to save you in return?"

"Ah, my dear! you might die a hundred times, and what difference would that make?" he cried, "except to leave me lonely till the time comes of my damnation?"

"You know nothing," said she. "I was educated in a school in Honolulu; I am no common girl. And I tell you, I shall save my lover. What is this you say about a cent? But all the world is not American. In England they have a piece they call a farthing, which is about half a cent. Ah! sorrow!" she cried, "that makes it scarcely better, for the buyer must be lost, and we shall find none so brave as my Keawe! But, then, there is France; they have a small coin there which they call a centime, and these go five to the cent or thereabout. We could not do better. Come, Keawe, let us go to the French islands; let us go to Tahiti, as fast as ships can bear us. There we have four centimes, three centimes, two centimes, one centime; four possible sales to come and go on; and two of us to push the bargain. Come, my Keawe! kiss me, and banish care. Kokua will defend you."

"Gift of God!" he cried. "I cannot think that God will punish me for desiring aught so good! Be it as you will, then; take me where you please: I put my life and my salvation in your hands."

Early the next day Kokua was about her preparations. She took Keawe's chest that he went with sailoring; and first she put the bottle in a corner; and then packed it with the richest of their clothes and the bravest of the knick-knacks in the house. "For," said she, "we must seem to be rich folks, or who will believe in the bottle?" All the time of her preparation she was as gay as a bird; only when she looked upon Keawe, the tears would spring in her eye, and she must run and kiss him. As for Keawe, a weight was off his soul; now that he had his secret shared, and some hope in front of him, he seemed like a new man, his feet went lightly on the earth, and his breath was good to him again. Yet was terror still at his elbow; and ever and again, as the wind blows out a taper, hope died in him, and he saw the flames toss and the red fire burn in hell.

It was given out in the country they were gone pleasuring to the States, which was thought a strange thing, and yet not so strange as the truth, if any could have guessed it. So they went to Honolulu in the *Hall* and thence in the Umatilla to San Francisco with a crowd of Haoles, and at San Francisco took their passage by the mail brigantine, the Tropic Bird, for Papeete, the chief place of the French in the south islands. Thither they came, after a pleasant voyage, on a fair day of the Trade Wind, and saw the reef with the surf breaking, and Motuiti with its palms, and the schooner riding within-side, and the white houses of the town low down along the shore among green trees, and overhead the mountains and the clouds of Tahiti, the wise island.

It was judged the most wise to hire a house, which they did accordingly, opposite the British Consul's, to make a great parade of money, and themselves conspicuous with carriages and horses. This it was very easy to do, so long as they had the bottle in their possession; for Kokua was more bold than Keawe, and, whenever she had a mind, called on the imp for twenty or a hundred dollars. At this rate they soon grew to be remarked in the town; and the strangers from Hawaii, their riding and their driving, the fine holokus and the rich lace of Kokua, became the matter of much talk.

They got on well after the first with the Tahitian language, which is indeed like to the Hawaiian, with a change of certain letters; and as soon as they had any freedom of speech, began to push the bottle. You are to consider it was not an easy subject to introduce; it was not easy to persuade people you were in earnest, when you offered to sell them for four centimes the spring of health and riches inexhaustible. It was necessary besides to explain the dangers of the bottle; and either people disbelieved the whole thing and laughed, or they thought the more of the darker part, became overcast with gravity, and drew away from Keawe and Kokua, as from persons who had dealings with the devil. So far from gaining ground, these two began to find they were avoided in the town; the children ran away from them screaming, a thing intolerable to Kokua; Catholics crossed themselves as they went by; and all persons began with one accord to disengage themselves from their advances.

Depression fell upon their spirits. They would sit at night in their new house, after a day's weariness, and not exchange one word, or the silence would be broken by Kokua bursting suddenly into sobs. Sometimes they would pray together; sometimes they would have the bottle out upon the floor, and sit all evening watching how the shadow hovered in the midst. At such times they would be afraid to go to rest. It was long ere slumber came to them, and, if either dozed off, it would be to wake and find the other silently weeping in the dark, or, perhaps, to wake alone, the other having fled from the house and the neighbourhood of that bottle, to pace under the bananas in the little garden, or to wander on the beach by moonlight.

One night it was so when Kokua awoke. Keawe was gone. She felt in the bed and his place was cold. Then fear fell upon her, and she sat up in bed. A little moonshine filtered through the shutters. The room was bright, and she could spy the bottle on the floor. Outside it blew high, the great trees of the avenue cried aloud, and the fallen leaves rattled in the verandah. In the midst of this Kokua was aware of another sound; whether of a beast or of a man she could scarce tell, but it was as sad as death, and cut her to the soul. Softly she arose, set the door ajar, and looked forth into the moonlit yard. There, under the bananas, lay Keawe, his mouth in the dust, and as he lay he moaned.

It was Kokua's first thought to run forward and console him; her second potently withheld her. Keawe had borne himself before his wife like a brave man; it became her little in the hour of weakness to intrude upon his shame. With the thought she drew back into the house.

"Heaven!" she thought, "how careless have I been – how weak! It is he, not I, that stands in this eternal peril; it was he, not I, that took the curse upon his soul. It is for my sake, and for the love of a creature of so little worth and such poor help, that he now beholds so close to him the flames of hell – ay, and smells the smoke of it, lying without there in the wind and moonlight. Am I so dull of spirit that never till now I have surmised my duty, or have I seen it before and turned aside? But now, at least, I take up my soul in both the hands of my affection; now I say farewell to the white steps of heaven and the waiting faces of my friends. A love for a love, and let mine be equalled with Keawe's! A soul for a soul, and be it mine to perish!"

She was a deft woman with her hands, and was soon apparelled. She took in her hands the change – the precious centimes they kept ever at their side; for this coin is little used, and they had made provision at a Government office. When she was forth in the avenue clouds came on the wind, and the moon was blackened. The town slept, and she knew not whither to turn till she heard one coughing in the shadow of the trees.

"Old man," said Kokua, "what do you here abroad in the cold night?"

The old man could scarce express himself for coughing, but she made out that he was old and poor, and a stranger in the island.

"Will you do me a service?" said Kokua. "As one stranger to another, and as an old man to a young woman, will you help a daughter of Hawaii?"

"Ah," said the old man. "So you are the witch from the eight islands, and even my old soul you seek to entangle. But I have heard of you, and defy your wickedness."

"Sit down here," said Kokua, "and let me tell you a tale." And she told him the story of Keawe from the beginning to the end.

"And now," said she, "I am his wife, whom he bought with his soul's welfare. And what should I do? If I went to him myself and offered to buy it, he would refuse. But if you go, he will sell it eagerly; I will await you here; you will buy it for four centimes, and I will buy it again for three. And the Lord strengthen a poor girl!"

"If you meant falsely," said the old man, "I think God would strike you dead."

"He would!" cried Kokua. "Be sure he would. I could not be so treacherous – God would not suffer it."

"Give me the four centimes and await me here," said the old man.

Now, when Kokua stood alone in the street, her spirit died. The wind roared in the trees, and it seemed to her the rushing of the flames of hell; the shadows tossed in the light of the street lamp, and they seemed to her the snatching hands of evil ones. If she had had the strength, she must have run away, and if she had had the breath she must have screamed aloud; but, in truth, she could do neither, and stood and trembled in the avenue, like an affrighted child.

Then she saw the old man returning, and he had the bottle in his hand.

"I have done your bidding," said he. "I left your husband weeping like a child; tonight he will sleep easy." And he held the bottle forth.

"Before you give it me," Kokua panted, "take the good with the evil – ask to be delivered from your cough."

"I am an old man," replied the other, "and too near the gate of the grave to take a favour from the devil. But what is this? Why do you not take the bottle? Do you hesitate?"

"Not hesitate!" cried Kokua. "I am only weak. Give me a moment. It is my hand resists, my flesh shrinks back from the accursed thing. One moment only!"

The old man looked upon Kokua kindly. "Poor child!" said he, "you fear; your soul misgives you. Well, let me keep it. I am old, and can never more be happy in this world, and as for the next –

"Give it me!" gasped Kokua. "There is your money. Do you think I am so base as that? Give me the bottle."

"God bless you, child," said the old man.

Kokua concealed the bottle under her holoku, said farewell to the old man, and walked off along the avenue, she cared not whither. For all roads were now the same to her, and led equally to hell. Sometimes she walked, and sometimes ran; sometimes she screamed out loud in the night, and sometimes lay by the wayside in the dust and wept. All that she had heard of hell came back to her; she saw the flames blaze, and she smelt the smoke, and her flesh withered on the coals.

Near day she came to her mind again, and returned to the house. It was even as the old man said – Keawe slumbered like a child. Kokua stood and gazed upon his face.

"Now, my husband," said she, "it is your turn to sleep. When you wake it will be your turn to sing and laugh. But for poor Kokua, alas! that meant no evil – for poor Kokua no more sleep, no more singing, no more delight, whether in earth or heaven."

With that she lay down in the bed by his side, and her misery was so extreme that she fell in a deep slumber instantly.

Late in the morning her husband woke her and gave her the good news. It seemed he was silly with delight, for he paid no heed to her distress, ill though she dissembled it. The words stuck in her mouth, it mattered not; Keawe did the speaking. She ate not a bite, but who was to observe it? for Keawe cleared the dish. Kokua saw and heard him, like some strange thing in a dream; there were times when she forgot or doubted, and put her hands to her brow; to know herself doomed and hear her husband babble, seemed so monstrous.

All the while Keawe was eating and talking, and planning the time of their return, and thanking her for saving him, and fondling her, and calling her the true helper after all. He laughed at the old man that was fool enough to buy that bottle.

"A worthy old man he seemed," Keawe said. "But no one can judge by appearances. For why did the old reprobate require the bottle?"

"My husband," said Kokua, humbly, "his purpose may have been good."

Keawe laughed like an angry man.

"Fiddle-de-dee!" cried Keawe. "An old rogue, I tell you; and an old ass to boot. For the bottle was hard enough to sell at four centimes; and at three it will be quite impossible. The margin is not broad enough, the thing begins to smell of scorching – brrr!" said he, and shuddered. "It is true I bought it myself at a cent, when I knew not there were smaller coins. I was a fool for my pains; there will never be found another: and whoever has that bottle now will carry it to the pit."

"O my husband!" said Kokua. "Is it not a terrible thing to save oneself by the eternal ruin of another? It seems to me I could not laugh. I would be humbled. I would be filled with melancholy. I would pray for the poor holder."

Then, Keawe, because he felt the truth of what she said, grew the more angry. "Heighty-teighty!" cried he. "You may be filled with melancholy if you please. It is not the mind of a good wife. If you thought at all of me, you would sit shamed."

Thereupon he went out, and Kokua was alone.

What chance had she to sell that bottle at two centimes? None, she perceived. And if she had any, here was her husband hurrying her away to a country where there was nothing lower than a cent. And here – on the morrow of her sacrifice – was her husband leaving her and blaming her.

She would not even try to profit by what time she had, but sat in the house, and now had the bottle out and viewed it with unutterable fear, and now, with loathing, hid it out of sight.

By-and-by, Keawe came back, and would have her take a drive.

"My husband, I am ill," she said. "I am out of heart. Excuse me, I can take no pleasure."

Then was Keawe more wroth than ever. With her, because he thought she was brooding over the case of the old man; and with himself, because he thought she was right, and was ashamed to be so happy.

"This is your truth," cried he, "and this your affection! Your husband is just saved from eternal ruin, which he encountered for the love of you – and you can take no pleasure! Kokua, you have a disloyal heart."

He went forth again furious, and wandered in the town all day. He met friends, and drank with them; they hired a carriage and drove into the country, and there drank again. All the time Keawe was ill at ease, because he was taking this pastime while his wife was sad, and because he knew in his heart that she was more right than he; and the knowledge made him drink the deeper.

Now there was an old brutal Haole drinking with him, that had been a boatswain of a whaler, a runaway, a digger in gold mines, a convict in prisons. He had a low mind and a foul mouth; he loved to drink and to see others drunken; and he pressed the glass upon Keawe. Soon there was no more money in the company.

"Here, you!" says the boatswain, "you are rich, you been always saying. You have a bottle or some foolishness."

"Yes," says Keawe, "I am rich; I will go back and get money from my wife, who keeps it."

"That's a bad idea, mate," said the boatswain. "Never you trust a petticoat with dollars. They're all as false as water; you keep an eye on her."

Now, this word struck in Keawe's mind; for he was muddled with what he had been drinking.

"I should not wonder but she was false, indeed," thought he. "Why else should she be so cast down at my release? But I will show her I am not the man to be fooled. I will catch her in the act."

Accordingly, when they were back in town, Keawe bade the boatswain wait for him at the corner, by the old calaboose, and went forward up the avenue alone to the door of his house. The night had come again; there was a light within, but never a sound; and Keawe crept about the corner, opened the back door softly, and looked in.

There was Kokua on the floor, the lamp at her side; before her was a milk-white bottle, with a round belly and a long neck; and as she viewed it, Kokua wrung her hands.

A long time Keawe stood and looked in the doorway. At first he was struck stupid; and then fear fell upon him that the bargain had been made amiss, and the bottle had come back to him as it came at San Francisco; and at that his knees were loosened, and the fumes of the wine departed from his head like mists off a river in the morning. And then he had another thought; and it was a strange one, that made his cheeks to burn.

"I must make sure of this," thought he.

So he closed the door, and went softly round the corner again, and then came noisily in, as though he were but now returned. And, lo! by the time he opened the front door no bottle was to be seen; and Kokua sat in a chair and started up like one awakened out of sleep.

"I have been drinking all day and making merry," said Keawe. "I have been with good companions, and now I only come back for money, and return to drink and carouse with them again."

Both his face and voice were as stern as judgment, but Kokua was too troubled to observe.

"You do well to use your own, my husband," said she, and her words trembled.

"O, I do well in all things," said Keawe, and he went straight to the chest and took out money. But he looked besides in the corner where they kept the bottle, and there was no bottle there.

At that the chest heaved upon the floor like a sea-billow, and the house span about him like a wreath of smoke, for he saw he was lost now, and there was no escape. "It is what I feared," he thought. "It is she who has bought it."

And then he came to himself a little and rose up; but the sweat streamed on his face as thick as the rain and as cold as the well water.

"Kokua," said he, "I said to you today what ill became me. Now I return to carouse with my jolly companions," and at that he laughed a little quietly. "I will take more pleasure in the cup if you forgive me."

She clasped his knees in a moment; she kissed his knees with flowing tears.

"O," she cried, "I asked but a kind word!"

"Let us never one think hardly of the other," said Keawe, and was gone out of the house.

Now, the money that Keawe had taken was only some of that store of centime pieces they had laid in at their arrival. It was very sure he had no mind to be drinking. His wife had given her soul for him, now he must give his for hers; no other thought was in the world with him.

At the corner, by the old calaboose, there was the boatswain waiting.

"My wife has the bottle," said Keawe, "and, unless you help me to recover it, there can be no more money and no more liquor tonight."

"You do not mean to say you are serious about that bottle?" cried the boatswain.

"There is the lamp," said Keawe. "Do I look as if I was jesting?"

"That is so," said the boatswain. "You look as serious as a ghost."

"Well, then," said Keawe, "here are two centimes; you must go to my wife in the house, and offer her these for the bottle, which (if I am not much mistaken) she will give you instantly. Bring it to me here, and I will buy it back from you for one; for that is the law with this bottle, that it still must be sold for a less sum. But whatever you do, never breathe a word to her that you have come from me."

"Mate, I wonder are you making a fool of me?" asked the boatswain.

"It will do you no harm if I am," returned Keawe.

"That is so, mate," said the boatswain.

"And if you doubt me," added Keawe, "you can try. As soon as you are clear of the house, wish to have your pocket full of money, or a bottle of the best rum, or what you please, and you will see the virtue of the thing."

"Very well, Kanaka," says the boatswain. "I will try; but if you are having your fun out of me, I will take my fun out of you with a belaying pin."

So the whaler-man went off up the avenue; and Keawe stood and waited. It was near the same spot where Kokua had waited the night before; but Keawe was more resolved, and never faltered in his purpose; only his soul was bitter with despair.

It seemed a long time he had to wait before he heard a voice singing in the darkness of the avenue. He knew the voice to be the boatswain's; but it was strange how drunken it appeared upon a sudden.

Next, the man himself came stumbling into the light of the lamp. He had the devil's bottle buttoned in his coat; another bottle was in his hand; and even as he came in view he raised it to his mouth and drank.

"You have it," said Keawe. "I see that."

"Hands off!" cried the boatswain, jumping back. "Take a step near me, and I'll smash your mouth. You thought you could make a cat's-paw of me, did you?"

"What do you mean?" cried Keawe.

"Mean?" cried the boatswain. "This is a pretty good bottle, this is; that's what I mean. How I got it for two centimes I can't make out; but I'm sure you shan't have it for one."

"You mean you won't sell?" gasped Keawe.

"No, sir!" cried the boatswain. "But I'll give you a drink of the rum, if you like."

"I tell you," said Keawe, "the man who has that bottle goes to hell."

"I reckon I'm going anyway," returned the sailor; "and this bottle's the best thing to go with I've struck yet. No, sir!" he cried again, "this is my bottle now, and you can go and fish for another."

"Can this be true?" Keawe cried. "For your own sake, I beseech you, sell it me!"

"I don't value any of your talk," replied the boatswain. "You thought I was a flat; now you see I'm not; and there's an end. If you won't have a swallow of the rum, I'll have one myself. Here's your health, and good-night to you!"

So off he went down the avenue towards town, and there goes the bottle out of the story.

But Keawe ran to Kokua light as the wind; and great was their joy that night; and great, since then, has been the peace of all their days in the Bright House.

Haoles – white people

Teach Me
To Dance

Kerryn Goldsworthy

I saw *Zorba the Greek* in the Capri Cinema in 1967 when I was fourteen. Julie and Helen and I went on the bus. I fell in love with Alan Bates, and we all cried. After everyone else had gone, Greek Helen danced down the red carpet slope of the centre aisle in the dim light of the cinema. Julie and I sat in our seats and watched. That was before I got my black dress.

Remember how often after that film came to Adelaide that a dance or a social or a party would end with everyone in a circle, doing Zorba's Dance? Kneecaps were kicked, at first, and people in high heels fell over. Later we all got quite good at it. At school there were a lot of Greek kids who had exotic names and brought unheard-of food to fetes: *baklava, kourabiethes, galataboureko.* They taught us how to dance, we played Alan Bates to their Anthony Quinn. ("Teach me to dance . . . will you?" "Did you say *dance?* Come on, my boy!") I had special lessons from Helen and knew a lot of fancy steps. She taught me the Greek alphabet, she taught me how to tell fortunes in a coffee cup: a letter, a journey, a troubled heart.

Two weeks after we saw that film I fell in love again, with a boy called George Santos who stayed beautiful for years. He looked at me over the top of his hamburger one winter afternoon in Waymouth Street and I was gone.

1967 was about the year that pantyhose became the norm in Adelaide. Most of us were just starting to get used to stockings and girdles and I don't mean wispy garter belts, I mean those step-in corset things that mummified you with elastic from just above your waist to halfway down your thighs. We threw them away.

Over your thick school pantyhose and black lace-up shoes, and pants and bra and petticoat and long-sleeved spencer, and white shirt and school tie, you pulled the belt of your box-pleat tunic tight and bloused the top up over the belt so that the pleats would fall straight on your hips and the hem would sit level and short over your knees. If you didn't, the tunic bagged at the bum and sagged down below the backs of your knees, and you looked like a dag. You wore your school jumper two sizes too big and brand new, and in the pocket of your blazer you carried a comb. You wore your beret at a specified angle I think we all hoped was French.

We studied the pictures of Twiggy and worked out that where makeup had once meant lipstick and rouge it now meant mascara and eyeshadow, and anyway rouge was called blusher, as you kept reminding your mother. Hair was like Mia Farrow's after she got it cut and they had to give Alison McKenzie brain surgery in *Peyton Place* to write her shorn head into the script. We sang 'Eleanor Rigby' and 'Scarborough Fair'.

School classes were streamed and in our class we had a reputation to keep up. The idea was to get good marks; but not too good, and without appearing to do any work. If you answered a lot of questions in class, or took more interest in anything than the curriculum required, you were weird. Either you were Attractive or you weren't, and if you were you spent the weekend doing your hair and talking to boys on the phone, and if you weren't you spent it doing your homework and going for long walks, bopping down the street with your transistor radio held up to your ear. Most of us walked hundreds of miles that year, up and down, up and down, haunted by the music of 1967 and wondering when everything would get better. We didn't know what history was, or beauty, or the world. At school I sat next to a girl called Anne Booker-Smith who spent hours drawing tidy maps of her future. She would marry a boy from Saint Peter's College (a few miles from our school) who would become a doctor and buy her a house in Unley Park (a few miles from our school) and they would have two sons called Justin and Daniel who would go to school at Saint Peter's College...

The most important thing about you was whether you were going out with anyone. That made you a star. If you had a chance to go out with any boy who didn't actually give you asthma, you took it and were grateful. After a decent interval you dropped the boy, or he dropped you, and then after another decent interval you started, if you were lucky, going out with someone else. Those were the rules. I went out with George Santos for five glorious weeks and got to kiss and look at him a lot before I got the chop. This blasted my whole existence, partly because of the lost status but mostly because in twenty years of looking at men I have still never seen anything as beautiful as George Santos was in 1967. His hair was black, his skin was gold, his mouth curled slightly upwards at one corner in the ghost of a James Dean sneer, and whenever I walk down North Terrace I see the boy he was, lying again in the sun on the grass in front of the War Memorial, propped up on one elbow looking at me, and behind him the great stone angel with the sword.

What turned my knees to water was that he was so strange. He was dark and different; he came from a foreign place, full of passion and history. And he made me think straight for the first time in my life about maleness, about the lures and riddles of a body that was nothing like my own. He was a man, and a Greek; he was another country.

So after five weeks of phone calls, and kisses in the movies, and coffees after school, George dropped me according to the rules, and three weeks after that there was a Junior Social at our 'brother school', my first real dance.

Julie and I confessed to each other at afternoon recess on the Friday of the dance that we were scared and we did not want to go. We had a teacher who specialised in girl talk (the importance of Personal Freshness; the ethics of trying to get out of gym by saying that you had your period), a woman who spoke seven languages and had fled with her parents from Europe as a teenager in 1939. She wore her hair too long, we thought, for a woman in her forties – almost down to her *shoulders* – and she wore strange dresses of a kind we had never seen our mothers in. To our horror, she wept openly whenever she heard the word Hitler, and as she taught us German with quite a lot of history thrown in, the word Hitler was sometimes hard to avoid. I now think that she was a beautiful and cultured woman, but we thought then that she was pushy, dowdy, hysterical and weird, and we feared her in a way that none of us understood.

She had given us one of her intimate little talks about the dance. It was important, she said, that we should dress and behave in a way that was pretty and modest, like ladies. It was important that we should be at ease with boys and talk to them intelligently on the topics of the day. It was important that we should mix, and not cling to one partner for the whole evening. And so on.

Julie and I discussed this homily at recess. Neither of us felt like ladies. Neither of us felt pretty, or modest, at least not in the way *She* meant. Boys made us both sweat, as a rule, and though we both knew a bit about the topics of the day we also knew that to talk intelligently about them to a boy was to invite a view of his retreating back. We were sure that nobody would ask us to dance at all, much less a suitable assortment of partners. We feared exposure; we feared being branded as the sort of girls boys didn't want to dance with, which meant we would grow up to be the sort of women men didn't want to marry, and what would we do then? We fretted about what to wear. Julie had two possible dresses but couldn't choose between them: the blue one with the collar, or the grey one with the lace? I was still growing out of everything I owned and wanted something new, and I had already spent every afternoon after school for a week trying on dress after dress and then tearing it off in despair, sometimes with tears stinging the backs of my eyes: this one made my legs look like milk bottles and that one made my hair look like an Army crewcut and one promising-looking red one turned my face a delicate pale green colour after I had put it on. I still didn't have anything to wear, and after school I headed heavily back to the shops for one last despairing search.

I nearly left the dress where it was. I'd never had a black dress before. My mother would say it was too old for me. On the other hand, I thought, lifting it absentmindedly from the rack, my mother also often said that I was too old for my own good. Only one of these two things, I said to her in my head as I walked to the dressing room, can possibly be true.

I hung it on the peg in the harsh light of the cubicle, which was pink and smelled warmly of other women's bodies. It was black velvet with a white taffeta collar and cuffs and three small buttons down the front of the short bodice. The sleeves had a big inverted pleat from the shoulder down the line of the arm, caught back tight and small again at the elbow by the wide pearly cuffs.

I took off the beret and the blazer, the new too-big jumper, the black lace-up shoes, the carefully belted tunic, the school tie, the white shirt and the long-sleeved spencer. I stood in my petticoat and pantyhose, looking in the mirror and hating it. No wonder George had fled, I thought; I looked like a bear cub whose mother had not yet licked it into shape. I took the black dress off the hanger and slipped it over my head.

One sunny winter afternoon many years later, when I had eaten nothing for two days and spoken no English for three weeks and was beginning to feel very strange, I turned a corner in the hall on the second floor of a *pensione* in Florence and saw at the end of the dim corridor, by a few stray beams of buttery light from the far window, a picture framed in scrolls of gilt and dust. In the half-dark I could see that it was the portrait of a woman, shadowy, still, remote; I saw the shape of her head and her straight unsmiling gaze. An old picture, a person lifted out of time; a woman, I thought, I would have rather liked to know. I moved forward for a closer look and felt the fine hairs rising at the back of my neck as the woman in the picture moved with me; it was not a portrait, but a mirror.

It was only the second time in my life that I had ever seen myself clearly, with no despair or pleasure or relief, only interest, like meeting the eye of a stranger on a train. The first time was that Friday afternoon in the dressing room when I looked up into the mirror from zipping and straightening my black dress and saw that some time in the last thirty seconds I had become the person I would be for the rest of my life. I had hoped as we all do unreasonably and everywhere for a Cinderella-like transformation, to be a success at the dance, but this was something very different. The Prince did not advance in my vision; he retreated, right out of sight. Whether the boys at the dance would find me Attractive in my new dress was not what I was thinking about as I looked into the mirror.

I was thinking I was free. The face of the girl in the mirror was neither pretty nor plain, but there, nudged into focus finally by a few yards of black velvet; on the Attractive Scale from one to ten she had somehow managed to disappear sideways off the graph, escape from the net of lines. She was telling me I had nothing now to fear or hope for from the dance; that I need draw none of the neat maps showing the doctor husband teaching Justin and Daniel how to be clean little snobs in Unley Park, for I would have no use for them; that I was free to wear my beret any way I wanted to and study as hard as I bloody well pleased. What I was not free of was my passion for George Santos and for men who would come after him, but that had nothing to do with the graph, or the map, or the dance. That went with learning, and knowledge, and the face above the black dress in the mirror.

Ballroom dancing, like unplucked eyebrows, baggy tunics and very high marks in exams, was daggy. The school ran occasional dispirited classes in it from time to time, but to attend them was not a thing that you did. So at my first dance I was one of the two hundred kids who stumbled round on the slippery floor of the school hall in our best clothes, trying not to fall over, trying to pretend that moving rhythmically as you held on tight to a partner of the opposite sex who you were right up against, touching, all the way down your front was something we all did every day. We were the young in one another's arms, and we were hopeless.

I think we had all expected to walk onto the dance floor and glide about, that all the precise steps would come to us as natural as breathing. We had been led to expect magic and ease, by movies and TV and fairy tales and songs and nineteenth-century fiction and old photographs of our parents, all dressed up at dances and looking pretty pleased about it and not anxious at all. I don't think it had ever occurred to any of us that Fred Astaire and Ginger

Rogers needed to rehearse. The cultural model for this kind of occasion was, say, a ballroom in nineteenth-century Paris where grown-up people, hung with emeralds or medals, spoke French and danced mazurkas under a constellation of shining chandeliers. We were two hundred fourteen-year-olds in a school hall with the chairs pushed back, with streamers and balloons in the school colours and a boy who was practising to be an electrician upstairs in the lighting booth; we were in a small city in post-Menzies Australia, the fag-end of those grey Edna Everage years that sent hundreds of artists of all kinds fleeing the country in boatloads, vowing never to return. And we couldn't dance.

George was there, carefully avoiding me and my gaze. Julie was there, raising her eyebrows meaningfully at me over the shoulders of various boys as we shuffled past each other on the dance floor, and seeking me out in the breaks to compare notes. Helen, like most of the Greek girls, was not allowed to go to dances – not even to this one where her brother Chris, a prefect, was in charge of the whole affair.

I suppose there must have been teachers there, to keep it all sober and chaste, but I don't remember seeing any. They wouldn't have had anything to worry about, or anything to do: Chris was there.

Prefects are supposed to be tall and blond and lordly and called David or Andrew, but Chris was small and Greek and irresistible. He fired the football team, carried the cricket team, dominated the debating team; he always got straight credits in all of his exams, and that year he played the part of the Pirate King in a cherry-coloured silk bandana tied pirate-fashion round his head, with a cream velvet tail-coat and mushroom-pink knee breeches and one gold earring, and when he first appeared on stage a lot of the younger mothers in the audience drew their breath in sharply and shifted in their seats. He was a flawless assimilator: he played Australian Rules, not soccer; he went out with Australian girls; he sang Gilbert and Sullivan; he got all A's in English. Teachers admired him, mothers adored him, fathers wondered about him.

He was, I now see, walking a very thin line indeed. With a reputation like that he could not afford to fail one test, to drop one catch, to sing one off-key note. He badly wanted, I think, neither to alienate himself from the Greek community nor to declare himself fully part of it. He knew his golden image was hard on Helen, for whom being younger and a girl had already made life quite difficult enough; he admired her and conspired with her, and he was far too intelligent to insult her with ostentatious Greek-brother protectiveness of a kind she did not need and could not, being Helen, have borne. He was seventeen, and with three of his friends he ran the dance without once raising his voice. Kids who tried to sneak outside in couples were gently steered back in, and kids who'd smuggled in beer or Brandavino were spotted and quietly sent home. The four of them wore their full school uniforms with their prefects' ties, just so there would be no mistake about who they were and what they were there for. They were only three years older than us, but they looked grown up, and formal, and remote.

Nobody asked either me or Julie for the supper dance and so we descended on the food together, grateful for each other's company and for the chance to eat without embarrassment anything we could get our hands on. Anne Booker-Smith, who had had more than her share of some brandy that her snotty boyfriend from the school orchestra had managed to get past the prefects (she hadn't cracked a boyfriend from Saint's yet, but she was working on it), dropped a piece of chocolate cake icing side down on Julie's pale grey dress and ran outside to be sick in the bushes. Andrew Carter, Julie reported, had dropped Robyn Donaldson just before the supper dance, and Robyn had cried. I replied that I knew for a fact that Sophie Lisgos and Dianne Marti were smoking in the girls' toilet, and that Kevin Boyle's new convent girlfriend had never had her hair cut in her whole life.

That was what the night was like, and that was fine with me. I loved gossip, and chocolate cake, and Julie, and I was still dazzled by the moment of enlightenment in the dressing room that afternoon: the event, the important thing, had already happened, hours before I arrived at the dance. I was sorry for the others, who looked as though they were still expecting it. But the lights came on and the band packed up and people began to drift out into the night, and still nobody had lost or found a glass slipper, danced in the moonlight, seen a stranger across a crowded room.

Then one of the boys who were packing up found a record that gave him an idea, and in a moment the first notes of Zorba's Dance

---

brought those of us who were left back onto the dance floor for the slow opening steps. We put our arms across each other's shoulders and smiled, Step-step-*kick*-step-step-step-*kick*-step, and the music went faster, and we got to the dangerous part where you actually leave the ground, jumping and kicking, faster and faster, shouting and laughing, and ties came off and makeup ran and hair came loose from its combs and pins and Chris burst through the line of arms and into the middle of the ring, dancing with his shirt open, coatless and barefoot and shouting in Greek, calling his friends by their true names to come into the ring and dance. Someone went running up the stairs and switched off all the lights, and then found Chris with the spotlight. Someone else turned the music up. Chris leaped and clapped and lunged and spun, alone in the golden spot, as if to deny all of his orderly skills and virtues, to throw off every fact about himself except that he was seventeen, and an athlete, and a Greek. One by one his friends joined in, throwing away their coats and ties and shoes and flinging themselves into the light, four of them dancing not in decorous couples and measured steps but like men and friends and because they really couldn't help it, in a wild joyful way that belonged to another place.

Women, when we each recall our own first dance, are traditionally supposed to remember things about ourselves: our triumphs and humiliations, how we dressed up and did our hair, when we arrived and who our partners were and how we felt when we came home. And I remember those things. But what I remember best is that ring of golden light, with men in it, and beauty, and the rest of us a great circle of watchers in the dark.

The New World

William Lane

In autumn she would always remember the old world. The air was thinner in autumn. The spaces between the houses grew. The leaves deepened and turned bitter colours. Dora pulled the cardigan about her, and stood by the sink, staring into the morning of the garden. Her toast and tea grew cold. In the street letterboxes sprouted like mushrooms. Windows once hidden by leaves were now exposed.

Then Dora heard what she had been waiting for – singing. A thin, high, voice, the frailest voice of a girl singing in the street. Dora caught her breath. The singing drew closer. The tendril of song wavered, trembled, then caught in her heart. She knew this song.

The girl passed by, head down on her way to school, watching her feet go shuck shuck shuck in the leaves.

Dora quickly took up her purse, eased her feet into her walking shoes, and quietly closed the door behind her. She began following the schoolgirl down the street.

Still singing, the girl cut across the park, leaving footsteps in the wet grass. Dora followed. They passed the swings and see-saws, beaded with little tears of dew. Dora's heart, intent upon the trembling line of melody the girl trailed, beat like a drum. The song was unstitching her note by note. She was unfurling beneath a different sky than this, the European sky of her childhood.

The girl passed through the school gate. The song faded as she climbed the school path. It was silenced behind glass doors.

Dora stood for a moment at a loss. The song went on in her mind. There was more of it, she knew, just beyond her memory. The girl always sang the beginning of the song, but never the end.

Opposite the school gates was the New World supermarket.

Dora took heart. She would do some shopping. She stroked the once furry sides of her purse. She must not cry, although she still could not find the end of the song. Before crossing the street she looked up. In this place the sky was so high and so blue. It frightened her.

Dora headed towards the arcade adjacent to the New World. She would go to the butcher's first. Skint the butcher would have just finished arranging his meat in the window. He did it so carefully, as if the different cuts were decorations.

The doors to the arcade opened mechanically, pneumatically, responding to the pressure of Dora's little feet. Inside it smelt of ink and ammonia – the newsagent, the doctor's surgery. This warmed Dora, these were the smells of shelter, of civilisation. And as the doors closed, she had the sensation of having her back covered. That sky gone.

The door to the doctor's surgery slid open as she passed, wafting an antiseptic slice of interior into the arcade. Dora averted her face. She was approaching the age of strokes. She pushed open the door of Skint's. Skint the butcher was standing in the shallow neon light, his back to the counter, repeatedly hacking at a side of beef – rather lack-lustrely, thought Dora. Desultory. Almost like a schoolboy pelting a tree or a body of water. Was Skint ill? Becoming aware of a customer's presence, he turned, and came shuffling to serve, the way the old butchers do. The tools of his trade, clustered on his thigh, jangled and padded.

"Ah, Mrs Lamb," said Skint, wiping his hands, "what can I do you today?"

Dora surveyed the exhibited meat.

She licked her lower lip.

The butcher's hands were dyed pink, and bunched, like frankfurters. They seemed so blurred, so numb, Dora wondered if they were capable of feeling. Or of touching.

"Cold outside?" asked Skint.

"Oh I was born in a colder country than this."

"I don't feel the cold either."

"Do they suffer?"

"Mrs Lamb?"

"Do the animals suffer?"

"I assure you the process is quick and painless. They don't feel a thing."

Skint clasped his hands afresh and tucked in his chin.

"That's a comfort," said Dora.

"They don't feel a thing," repeated Skint. His eyes travelled towards the shop window.

People were walking hurriedly beyond the glass, head-down past the butcher's. A thread of melody like a nerve was running back through Dora's mind. Bells jingled in the stalls of a market. Cattle lowed and steamed. Hooves and feet stamped, whips cracking. The long, luxurious morning pisses of the cattle.

They don't feel a thing.

"Sometimes I see them, you know," said Dora, "at night – the cattle trucks. Full of cattle. Do they only transport them at night? The stench of it, I remember it. I remember it from when I was a girl. And not only cows. Not only – cows."

The butcher wiped one red hand back and forth upon his apron. He began whistling.

Dora suddenly turned and made for the door. She pushed and pushed – it would not open. She began shaking it violently. Skint was talking to her, but she could not hear, her ears were full of other sounds. He had to come around from behind the counter, and open the door for her – it only needed a pull, not a push – before she could flee his shop.

Dora gasped in the unbutchered air outside. She had become a little girl again, watching the cows being slaughtered. No, not the cows. Although she had seen that. A man. Many men, against the whitewashed wall, the village wall. Now she remembered the song the schoolgirl had been singing, all of it, from beginning to end. The men had been singing it, in unison, before the wall turned red, and their souls floated up above the thatch.

Then right before her, in the middle of the arcade, a child was crying, turning and turning, its face drawn and crimson, distended in despair.

"It's crying," said Dora. "What of it?" snapped a woman nearby, pushing letters into a letterbox. She identified herself as the mother by walking to the child and hitting it, shopping bags sliding along her arm, pummelling the child one by one. The child's mouth opened and shut.

"It's suffering," cried Dora, kneeling.

"It's doing no such thing," shouted the woman, now looking frightened. "Don't touch my child!"

The girl was dragged off across ox-blood tiles, leaving Dora kneeling with arms akimbo. She shook her head, stood, and was ushered back into the car park by nervously obliging doors.

Outside a choir of children was singing distantly in one of the neighbouring school buildings. Joining other voices in twilight, over dark sloping fields. High girls' voices, harmonising without thought, moving as a body across the harvested land.

Dora crossed the car park hurriedly, making towards the New World. Another set of automatic doors opened to tinselly, trebly music. Dora proceeded directly to the Frozen Goods. She liked freezing things. Then the canned goods, every day she bought more canned goods, they lasted years.

She bought as much as she could carry.

In the confectionery aisle she realised the ancient melody in her head had been buried under piped pop music. She could not remember it if she tried.

Dora felt better. Outside the sun was beginning to warm the car park. I should apologise to Skint right now, she thought, I'll have to face him sooner or later. It's always wise to be on good terms with your butcher. Your meat depends upon it.

"Ah! Mrs Lamb," said Skint, much as he had previously. "Feeling better?" Skint regarded his contrite customer dolefully.

"Yes, thank you," admitted Dora, flushing, "I feel so much better now. I must apologise for earlier. I wasn't myself. Now, can I have a look at that rack of lamb?"

Skint sheathed his knife. He took up the cleaver.

He brought her an eight-fingered side. "I was saving you this one," he announced.

Dora inspected the fatty margins laced with vessels, testing the texture of the meat in her mind, and the webby intervals between the bone.

"Yes, it looks lovely," she said. "Thank you, Mr Skint."

Skint sliced off some of the fat, whistling brightly.

"I knew you'd be back," he said, wrapping up the meat, whistling.

Striker

Matthew Fitt

Luke's twelfth grade Historical Biology teacher, Mr Seltzer, wis in slaver over-drive. His heid filled the screen m the comer o Luke's bedroom afore it wis replaced by a pictur o a green beastie. "This is a visual of the South American tree frog," havered Mr Seltzer, "which was made extinct in the year 2035. Check out its colouring and shape. What does it remind you of? Enter a thought in your lapbooks now."

Luke thocht the Sooth American puddock looked like Mr Seltzer's pus but he didnae enter *that* intae his lapbook. He didnae dare. Mr Seltzer wisnae extinct, altho he wis in Chicago. Chicago wis thoosans o kms awa fae Dumfries but if whit he did tae puir Rui Roshinhio fae Brazil.

Rui pit thegither a repro model o a lang deid member o the ape faimlie cryed an Orangutang an stuck a graphic o the Historical Biology teacher's heid on tap o the monkey's boady, syne e-mailed it tae aw bis clessmates' screens roon the planet. When ane ended up by mistake in Seltzer's doocot at the WestSchool main office in Chicago, Auld Seltzy went radgie supernova. He poued the plug on Rui's WestSchool link-up in Brazil an consequently on wee Rui's future wi WestCo. If Luke ever did onythin tae guddle up his ain future wi WestCo, Luke's faither wid kill him.

Luke tholed the lesson aboot puddocks that yaised tae lowp aboot in Sooth America tae the end. Altho he aye cawed canny aroon Mr Seltzer, he switched aff the screen afore he'd heard his hamework. He couldnae help hissel. It didnae maitter if the WestSchool attendance computer registered him slippin awa early or no. He could aye blame it on a pouer-cut an if the hamework exercise wis a sair yin, his baw-heid neebor, Massimo in Italy, wid soon enough e-mail him up fur the answers an he could git the hamework aff him. Luke couldna gie a fleein giga-byte if the schule kent or no. It wis Seturday. Glesga were at hame tae Madrid. An naethin else on the planet maittered.

He'd been up tae hi-doh aw moarnan, chappin the leg o his chair wi his guttie, enterin glaikit answers tae simple questions, his mind hotchin wi crosses, penalties an goals insteid o makkin notes aboot barkit bauchled wee beasties. Luke thocht maist o thaim were that boaky-lookin it wis a guid joab they were deid onywey. Luke didna care aboot onythin but Glesga an Madrid. He pit oot auld Seltzy's puddock-like geggie pronto an cleared his desk. He had better things tae dae. He wis gaun roon tae Flynn's fur tae watch the big gemm on Flynn's new CyberStation.

Luke's ma wis doon the stair goin the messages in the front room. She looked like she wis daein some kind o auld-farrant war dance or the mating ritual o the extinct Euro-Asian peacock he'd been learnin aboot the ither day. He chapped the 'pause' button on the faimlie's scartit auld oot-dated HelpMaster system that aye gied Luke a riddie every time ony o his pals come in the hoose an seen it. His ma stapped hauf-wey doon the Syntho-veggie section an momentarily left the Virtual Supermarket environment tae hear fae her son.

"Hurry, Luke," she sayd, in that mealie-moothed NewCal English wey she had that made Luke's stomach lowp like a garbage mixer. "There's a special on frozen whale this week-end and you know how tense your father gets if he hears he's missed out on some gourmet beluga."

Luke wis sair tempted tae hit the 'play' button an let his ma pauchle on doon the supermerkit dreel tae the great muckle gless bunkers o synthetic sea meat. Fur a stert, she wis aboot as bauchled as the muckle great HelpMaster unit, no juist her claes or her hair, but the wey she stood. The wey she wis. Secondly tho, the thocht o her beatin aw the ither wifies an hoose husbands tae the stots o whale meat an so guaranteein an oor or twa wi his faither bein no sae radge as usual wis a muckle incentive tae. His faither had taen the stress shuttle tae Holland fur the efterninn fur a roond o buddy gowf wi his WestCo workmates as pairt o the company's rage management program. He widna be back til late.

Luke didna hurl his mither back intae shoppin limbo. "I'm away to Dermot Flynn's," he sayd, shauchlin taewards the door. "I'll be back at eighteen."

"Not a minute later," his ma replied. "I'm re-microing yesterday's stork burgers and if you're good, your father may share some beluga with you."

Luke wis near oot the door.

"Do you have enough euros on your card?" she spiered him. Luke's credit panel wis unusually fou o spankies the nou.

"Ay," he flung back intae the room an turned tae leave.

"Luke!" He heard his mither's kenspeckle lug-nippin high-pitched skraik an turned back. "That is not how we speak in this house and certainly not what you learn at WestSchool. I will ask you again. Do you have enough money?"

"Yes, mother," Luke replied wi a heavy mooth. His mither didnae like him speakin Auld. "I'll be home at six, mother." A crouse wee victory smile spreid across her triple x foondation cream beclartit cheeks like a crack openin up in Earthquake America an Luke pushed 'play'. She kerried on mimin her wey doon the supermerkit aisle. Luke quit the hoose.

Flynn steyed in ane o the big hooses up the brae. Flynn's faither had an auld ermy telescope an when they were bairns, Luke an Flynn had spent oors in the tap room o the hoose glowerin across the Irish Sea an keekin richt intae shop windaes in the hert o Belfast. Whiles they had been able tae mak oot the clouds o reek an smog that hingit owre the twin-city conurb o Manchester an Liverpool. But there were nane o thaim bairns ony mair. They were stieve strappin junior adults nou. Luke an Flynn had ither things tae play at.

The brae tae Flynn's hoose wis a sair pech an Luke trauchled up it on the flittin sidewalk. He hirpled throu the avenue o birk trees

but the wey she stood.

that led up tae Flynn's hoose an rang the bell. A security pad flipped oot at him as he stood hechin at the front door. He registered his haun-prent wi the hoose computer an chapped his fowre-letter password intil the keyboard. The door opened an Flynn wis on the ither side.

"Hey, dude," Flynn sayd, hucklin a haunfou o blond hair awa fae his fore heid. "Gemm's stertin. Hurry ben." Luke follaed him throu the lang white ivory-tile lobby he yaised tae imagine wis the stert o the road tae heaven, an doon intae the basement o the muckle five-storey hoose. Flynn's liquid disc music center wis skelpin oot Track 8 fae Gooseberry's new dog vid 'The Dress is Easy'. The Hammerslam drum beat stottit roon the reid brick basement space. Luke could feel his bluid stert tae gowp in his veins. He wis chokin tae see Flynn's new Station. If it wis hauf as intense as Flynn had described it til him owre the face-phone, then this wis really gonnae be somethin tae wet his punders fur.

The Station wis skelp-new. It sat on its lane at the faur end o the basement. Luke could mak oot twa muckle reid memory kists as braid an as big as coffins. They were jined in the middle by a siller cube. Luke kent thon wis the reality engine. Thon wis where the magic happened. "Where's the suit, Flynn? How do I put it on?" Luke couldnae dam the torrent o havers skitterin oot his mooth.

"Yo, radge person. Tak a chill pill. Chow a caw-canny-granny-sooker, eh, an haud yir wheesht twa seconds. Captain Wilson Flynnsky is here and will give what you need." Flynn wis ettlin tae be cool but Luke kent his doh wis as high as his. Flynn hadnae been virtual witness at a live gemm yet. The haill thing wis new tae thaim baith. The blethers soon come skooshin oot o Flynn tae. As he poued Luke by the airm owre til the equipment, he stertit haverin aboot his da.

Flynn's faither worked fur MedCal Worldwide. He wis a surgeon. Fifteen meenits afore Flynn wis alloued tae git his clatty wee hauns on the new equipment, faither Flynn, fae the basement o his hoose in Dumfries, had been up tae his oxters in a hert-bypass op on a patient papped oot on a theatre bed ten thoosan kms awa in Singapore's Windsor Memorial Hospital, slicin throu veins an arteries wi a remote virtual scalpel. Luke didnae care. He wis cauld tae talk o Flynn's faither. He micht hae been cuttin a daud o biled ham fur his denner.

Luke wisnae intressit. This Station had the SportsInYourFace channel that naebody this side o Moscow could git an Luke waantit in.

Flynn redd up Luke Wi the richt gear. He made Luke pit on an electronic semmit. Juist as he wis gittin yaised tae the slidderie feel o the vest on his skin, Flynn slaistered a haunfou o conductor gel roon the side o Luke's heid. "Oyah," gret Luke. The jeely wis cauld. "That's right, ma wee keekie-mammy," sayd Flynn, dichtin his ain napper wi the gel. "Just

like in the Holywood CD-ROMS when the bad guy gets the chair."
Flynn skirled owre tae a postal kist wi the delivery-hap still on an
returned wi twa VR helmets. Luke pit his on but left the bleck gless
vizor up. Flynn did the same syne went back tae the kist, he kerried
owre twa gowden boxes. Luke rived the box open. Inside wis a pair
o gowden buits, glintin, keekin in the hauf lich to the room. He pit
thaim on. The buits wis as licht as air.

"A minute to three. You ready?" sayd Flynn.

"Yes," replied Luke an mindin his mither, added, "Ay."

Flynn chapped the word 'ready' intae the command panel.
Luke felt a skitter o energy ripple throu the electrodes attached tae
his heid. His wame rummled wi excitement. A lump the size o ane
o his faither's Slazengers stuck in his thrapple. Flynn hut the 'play'
button an the reality engine come tae life wi an electronic pech.
Luke an Flynn snapped thair vizors doon.

Bleckness.

A buzzin in the lug.

Pain stobbin doon the left side o the boady. A mind-shooglin
sense o wechtlessness an the urgent need tae boak. Mair bleckness.
Ainlie bleckness. A pitmirk prospect unrelieved by ony licht. An
the stomach, the geggie, the boak-bag gaun roon like a car wheel.

Fur a second, Luke waantit it stapped. This virtual world wisnae
richt. It didnae feel guid. He waantit tae gang back tae reality. He
waantit Flynn fur tae turn it aw aff, shaw him tae the nearest
restroom, funn a shunkie an pit his heid doon it. But sic sairness
soon passed. The mirk curtain poued back an Luke wis deeved by
the stotter o buits on concrete. A voice kittled in his lug.
FRAGOLA, ROJAS, HAMMER, BOROVSKY . . . a licht appeared
up aheid o him, the clatter o studs cawin him forrit . . . WOLF, LE
MAN, VAN HALEN. Luke bielded his een. A bleeze brichter nor
the sun stumoured him. A rummle-tummle orchestra o voices
drooned the ane in his lug an drookit aw his senses. He felt hissel
run oot ontae the pitch. A firework skitit by him. Stieve airms
swung bricht muckle multi-coloured flags throu the reekin air. Big
men wi lang sleekit bleck hair stood in a raw on either side o him wi
thair hauns ahint thair backs, Glesga in reid, Madrid in white.
SOLDAT, LAURENTIS, VANINIO. The wee voice focht tae be
heard owre the loud, rauchle yins. AND GRAY. The match

commentator feenished the team leet wi the ainlie Scottish player in the Glesga side an a rair riz roon the groond like a plump o thunner.

"Luke. Yo, Luke." Luke heard his ain name cawed oot owre aw the din. "Luke. Up here." Next thing Luke kent he wis a hunner metres up hingin owre the stadium in mid air wi Flynn hingin alangside him. "Hey, thought ye'd like that. I programmed you to come out with the teams." Luke keeked doon. He could see the haill arena. The players had skailed fae the touch line an were spreidin owre the pitch tae skelp practice baws intae their ain goals. Luke had a fear o hichts but he wisnae tellin Flynn that. "Can we try the main stand?" he spiered, pointin doon at the seated area ahint the Glesga goal, hotchin wi a rammy o boadies. "That's so lame," replied Flynn. "Pick a player. Let's do POV. I'll go Rojas. Who do you want?" Luke waled oot Gray an in a second he wis back doon at pitch level, seein awthin fae Gray's point o view.

The gemm stertit an Gray got the baw furst. Luke felt a thrill slidder throu him. Gray took the baw roon a Madrid player. The Spaniards were in white an Luke saw a white-sleeved elba jouk towards Gray's face. Luke flenched, shuttin baith his een. He opened thaim again a second later. Gray aye had the baw an wis hechin an pechin at full speed doon the weeng. Gray keeked up an in thon hauf-second Luke experienced Gray's realisation that a pass wis on tae Rojas tae the left o him. Luke willed his man tae chap the baw owre the turf but afore he could pou back his foot, the white jersey o Zenga, the muckle-boukit Madrid sweeper, wis scuddin across his path. Luke felt a shairp pain in his ankle an Gray wis skitin neb-doon on the gress.

"Why didn't you pass, you loser?" Flynn's voice nipped him. "I was clear through on goal."

Luke gied his pal the deef lug. He wisnae enjoyin this as muckle as he thocht he wid. This wis gittin owre real. Flynn's faither's reality engine could reproduce a haill stadium. It could mak him feel every scart an skelp a player took. If a player went doon wi a terrible clatter, the thing micht be able tae replicate a gammy leg or burst heid on him. Luke tried tae soond bored. "Where else can we go with this?"

"Let's try the executive box," suggestit Flynn. "See if we can catch any of the players' girlfriends." Luke's mooth went dry. He'd seen some o thir women on terrestial tv. Maist o thaim hirpled aboot on the catwalk in cutty sarks an high heels. They were shiny like new aipples, thair lips reid an thair een bricht. Lookin at thaim gart Luke's legs turn tae jeely. He stuttered tae Flynn that thon wis a guid idea but when the pair rematerialised owre the directors' box, they funn thair road barred. The virtual programmers had wired in a bleck-oot code forenent the executive suite tae bield the high heid-yins an thair bonnie freens fae clarty-mindit wee boys like Flynn an Luke. The twa lads wis scunnered. They could mak oot neither breist or hurdie. Aw they could jalouse wis a stushie o shaddas an bogles flittin ahint a fug o static an distortion.

"I want a goal," announced Flynn. "My chip says that a score from Glasgow is imminent."

"Who's most likely to get it?" Luke wis eident nou tae hurl himself back intae the gemm tae mak up fur bein feert earlier an fur no gittin tae keek doon some model's blouse. "I'm going to go POV again."

"Cool the beans, kid." Flynn spoke wi a crabbit edge til his voice. There wisnae usually mony goals scored in a ticht gemm like this an Flynn waantit tae be in the richt place at the richt time if onybody hut the back o the net. The statistics computer wis whusperin in his lug that Rojas wid likely score in the next twa-three meenits. "The chip's tellin me Gray's about to put one away. You go POV on Gray for a while. I'll take - let me see now - och, I'll take Rojas." Flynn wis a canny liar.

"Thanks," replied Luke, excitement kittlin ben in his hert like a fire. Luke thocht himsel owre intae Gray's boady. He kent that the player had nae idea he wis there. A shoogle o unpleasant thochts skitit throu him as he imagined the same thing happenin tae him. He widnae like a stranger inhabitin his boady, even if it wis juist fur a gemm o fitba.

A dunt on the heid brocht him back fae his dwam. Gray had juist heidered the baw doon tae Le Man an Le Man wis chasin aff tae the ither side o the park. Gray wis miles awa fae the goal. He wis huckled forby. Luke wis aware o the semm pain fae that roch challenge earlier, stobbin awa doon in his ankle. Altho Luke had nae control owre Gray's movement, he could feel exactly whit the player felt. An Gray seemed tae be aboot tae cowp owre fae exhaustion. He didnae hae the strenth tae tie his am shuin never mind run the lenth o the pitch tae the penalty box. Luke wis vexed. This couldna be richt. Mibbe Flynn's statistics wis wrang. Gray widnae even score in the next oor. Luke's auld granny had mair chance o grabbin a goal than him.

Luke took in the furious action up aheid. Gray wis caucht in defence an wis pechin his wey back up the pitch. The gemm burled roon the pitch at haliket speed. There aye seemed tae be a rammy o players in orbit roon the baw, flittin across the park like a twister. Luke watched as a wide player floated a great cross in fae the corner flag. Rojas lowped up owre the shooders o the Spanish defence an skelped the baw wi his heid strecht at the Madrid goal. The keeper couldnae git aff his wrang fit an soon the baw wis a flash o white wheechin past his feckless raxin fingirs. The haill stadium wheesht. Luke held his tae, realisin wi a shairp pou on his hert that Flynn had pauchled him o a goal. He boued his heid, his lugs soon ringin wi Flynn's snochterie voice.

"Damn," it said. Luke keeked up. Rojas hadnae scored. Luke saw the baw stot back aff the crossbar. He lauched. Serves the spoilt wee eejit right, thocht Luke, but afore he could interface wi Flynn an tell him where tae stick his keechie machine, he funn himsel pechin an hoastin fae sudden exertion. Gray, he jaloused, had stertit tae run.

The baw had skitit aff the crossbar at sic a pace, it had rebounded tae near the hauf-wey line. The Spanish defence had forgot aw aboot Gray an naebody wis near him when he picked the baw up. As he cairried the baw forrit on his feet, Luke could sense Gray mak his choice. Rojas wis aff-side, Le Man an Wolf baith marked oot the gemm. The ainlie road in wis Route Wan, strecht throu the middle. Luke felt Gray's hert chap louder at his chist. He experienced the player tak in a lang lung-fou o air. Awthin disappeared forby the road tae goal. Luke wis nae langer aware o the rummle o the fans, nor could he tell if the loud drummin in his lugs wis Gray's hertbeat or his.

The next five seconds wis as fast as a slap in the ja. Gray skinned yin defender. The baw sklaffed aff the legs o anither. Zenga, the muckle, reid-beardit sweeper, flung himsel at Gray but Gray kept the heid an jouked roon him. When the Spanish keeper come chairgin oot, Gray wis the lown centre o a gallus storm. Sweat run aff his neb. His hair hingit doon owre yin ee. He keeked up. The keeper's hauns wis near gruppin the baw. Gray's rigbane tensed. He brocht his fit doon shairp unner the baw an it spun up, lowped the keeper an drapped richt intae the yawnin mooth o the goal.

WILLIE GRAY PUTS GLASGOW AHEAD. A BEAUTIFUL PENALTY BOX LOB STUNS THE MADRID PLAYERS. THE AULD FIRM FAITHFUL GO WILD BEHIND US HERE IN THE COMMENTARY POD. Luke couldnae credit the noise aroon him. His brain literally stapped as a wave o pure soond, whipped up by the hot braith fae seeventy thoosand thrapples, rattled his banes an biled the bluid inside his veins. His hert soared skyward. He forgot aw aboot Gray an alloued himsel tae believe it wis him lowpin owre the advertisin boards takkin the accolades o the Glesga crowd. LUKE PATERSON, he heard as he flung his reid Glesga FC sark intae the main stand, HAS REALLY SET THIS GAME ALIGHT. LUKE PATERSON HAS SCORED AN INCREDIBLE GOAL. MADRID HAVE NO ANSWER TO THE MIGHTY LUKE PATERSON.

"Luke Paterson, ya wee bampot." Luke could hear Flynn fizzin away in the background. "That was my goal. You took my goal." Luke didna care. He'd scored his goal. He kent nou whit it wis like tae mak thoosans o people chant yir name. "Paterson, you're outa here, boy. I'm through with you." Flynn's greetin voice didna maitter. Luke couldna hear it onywey. He wid git nae higher than this. It didnae come ony better than this.

Syne awthin went deid. Luke wis back in Flynn's faither's basement again. Flynn had cut him oot o the gemm. Luke liftit the vizor fae aff his face. Flynn wis staunin aside him, cairryin on wi the match on his ain. Luke kent the script weel. His posh pal did this fae time tae time. It wis Flynn's baw an Luke wisnae gittin tae play. Luke poued aff aw the virtual witness gear an shawed himsel oot the hoose.

Tae mak the warm feelin ben in his hert last as lang as he could, Luke went hame by a road he didnae usually tak. It took him roon by the high flats an alang the side o the river.

A puckle o laddies wis blooterin a fitba tae each anither on a square o gress. They were aw guid. Luke wis surprised they werenae watchin the big gemm. As he hurried alang past thaim, he thocht o the sheer gallusness o Gray's wee chip owre the Spanish goalkeeper an re-run in his heid the radge celebrations o the Glesga FC fans. Luke wis in mid-dauner throu his dwam when somethin fremmit hut aff his leg. It wis a baw.

"See's it back, eh?" ane o the laddies cryed owre til him. Luke keeked up. He saw he wis near the twa jaikets set oot on the gress fur goals. He realised he wis in exactly the same position as he wis when Gray chipped Cabuta. He kent whit tae dae. He stepped up tae the baw, poued his left fit back an brocht his guttie doon hard on the grund. The baw spun up, wheeched throu the air at an unco angle, stottit aff the grund aboot twinty feet fae the goals an run awa doon intae the river. The laddies went daft. Ane skelped owre tae the river bank tae retrieve the baw. The lave come breengin up tae Luke wi thair een as haurd as nieves. Luke turned an tried tae hirple awa, his face as reid as Willie Gray's shirt. Luke's mooth went dry.

He had never kicked a baw in his life.

Glossary

auld-farrant – old fashioned; *cawed canny* – went carefully; *clauty-mindit* – dirty minded; *cowp owre* – fall over; *drookit* – soaked; *dwam*- dream; *eident* – keen, determined; *ettlin* – intending; *fremmit* – strange; *glaikit* – stupid; *gowden buits* – golden boots; *haud yer wheesht* – keep quiet; *hechin an pechin* – huffing and puffing; *jalouse* – work out, discern; *kenspeckle* – easily noticed; *lowp* – leap; *muckle-boukit* – big-built; *puddock* – frog; *radgie* – mad; *riddie* – a red face, to blush; *shauchlin* – shuffling; *syne* – then; *tholed* – suffered; *thrapple* – throat.

Black Hole

Geraldine Stowe

The engines hummed with a rhythmic monotony as the convict ship *Minerva* made its solemn way through the blackness of space.

Ailssa stared through the porthole of her capsule as the interplanetary craft sped smoothly away from Estra. Days ago the star colony had shone with a luminous presence right outside the steel circle of her crystal window, but now it had shrunk to the size of a pinhead. The distant galaxies and stellar clusters winked and blinked at Ailssa from their dark canvas like sparks from a child's bonfire, and she could no longer be sure which one of those pulsating lights was Dante's new home.

Dante, her only child. Dante, the mutant.

The realisation that she would not see Dante again brought Ailssa close to panic. She fought her terror, choking on it. Surrounded by the outer reaches of empty space she felt more alone than she had ever felt before.

In most of the five hundred capsules on board the Hillsborough the occupants had already turned in for the journey. Earth was four light years away, and although each capsule was fitted with a macro walloven which provided every kind of meal at the twist of a dial, and a virtual reality telescreen which ensured non-stop visual, audio and tactile entertainment, most people preferred to sleep. They had lowered themselves onto the cribs in the steel cylinders, tightened the webbing belts and pressed the red plastic buttons. Anaesthesia cones had descended noiselessly from above to send the human beings gently to sleep. The two sides of each cylinder had closed like a nut, silver in the phosphorescent light of the capsule, before rolling silently away to rock easily on a sea of liquid helium in the freezing chambers. The power in the capsule had then shut down.

"This is evensong for the tenth day of October, 2305," announced the recorded voice of the pilot. "There are thirty-seven of you still operating on lifespans. It is my duty to remind you that this time is irreclaimable."

Ailssa wondered why they bothered to keep to Earth's calendar. What did it matter whether it was morning or evening since they were travelling through an everlasting night?

"If you wish to join the sleepers you must first deposit all traces of your past in the incinerator."

Ailssa held the photos of Dante in her hands and prepared for another wakeful night. She had carried the pictures with her for years, collecting them, treasuring them and hiding them carefully in her clothing. She could not summon up the courage to part with them just yet.

"The incinerator will be closing down in five minutes," came the metallic voice from the intercom. "To embrace the future you must first eradicate the past."

The picture of Dante as a baby was her favourite. It had been clear from the day he was born that he was not the same as other children. He was large and clumsy. His skin had an olive cast to it and his body looked smooth and bald. Ailssa had loved the naked creature from the start but as she held her son tightly in her arms she had felt a shadow like that of a large black bird fall across her life.

"What is it?" breathed Zadok, frightened by the sound of her voice.

"I do not know."

"Where has it come from?"

"It is ours, Zadok. It is our own flesh and blood."

He had refused to believe her at first. He had stormed and ranted. He had torn the coloured glassworks from the walls and broken them on the slate floor. He had accused her of being unfaithful and had shouted abuse until he had collapsed on the pallet and Ailssa had comforted him until he had fallen asleep, exhausted and frightened. How could she forget? And how she wished Zadok was with her now as she made her lonely journey back to Earth.

"The incinerator is closing down for the evening. Programs for the eleventh day of October 2305 appear on your screens on channel eighty-seven. All cybergames are operational. Have a nice night."

The dull click was followed by a smooth hiss as the hermetic shield slid across the intercom membrane.

Dante was an intelligent boy. He knew he was different from the other children. Ailssa had watched him grow with alarm. She never got used to the stares of those around her when she took him to the magnetopark or the hypermarket. "Stop it," she felt like screaming. "Please!" She had a picture of him now, wearing his plastic jumpsuit with the insignia and high blue collar. He was smiling up at Zadok, who was holding him by the hand. It was the day he started school, and there was just a hint of uncertainty in those wide green eyes and along the line of his mouth.

Ailssa was to see that look grow more hooded and desperate as the weeks progressed, but what could she do?

The law was the law.

She suffered for him. Some days he would arrive home with his face bloodied and his body cut and bruised. She could hardly look at the picture now without feeling the pain of that early separation.

Ailssa walked across to the walloven, set the dial, and twisted open the perspex door. She took out a hot moulded pastry nugget with a regular meat filling. It had been Dante's favourite. She moved idly to the telescreen and flicked it on.

"Good evening." The voice seemed to come from a long way away and sounded like warm winds blowing through desert caves. "This is the official communication service of planet Earth operating throughout the metagalaxy..." Ailssa chewed at the nugget, tasting little. A thin music poured from the telescreen. A black flag appeared with the words 'Strength at all Times'.

The music faded. "Your programs for tonight..."

The law was clear about mutants. Children born with a disability or physical handicap had to look after themselves from school age onwards. It was against the law to protect them in public.

A mutant with survival skills, however, was allowed to stay on the planet. It was the twenty-fourth century. Earthlings were not savages.

If a mutant was not able to look after himself he was deported to Estra, a distant star in the galaxy of Centaurus. A primitive settlement had been set up there several generations ago. Convict ships made the journey frequently, travelling at a hundred kilometres a second through the black holes in space that the interplanetary navigators referred to as wormholes.

Ailssa stared at a third photo of Dante. This was the last picture she had of him. It had been taken on that terrible evening when his classmates had come for him. There were twelve or more of them that night. They had waited for him in the gathering dusk and ambushed him on the main esplanade. He was sixteen. They broke his left leg. And then they broke his right. As Dante clawed his way along the blacktop towards his home the group of them followed, ironically cheering him on.

"No contact has been made. In such a case we convert to auto-select . . ."

What happened next was a nightmare. Zadok saw his broken son on the roadway and his reason left him. "Get back!" shouted Dante. "Please dad!" but Zadok did not hear him. He ran at the milling mob, howling with anger, and they fell upon him. He was borne away on a tide of hysteria. It was the last Ailssa saw of him.

The deportation order arrived the following day.

The telescreen had made its own program selection and was showing a comedy about family life with the sound turned down. The laughter was recorded and sounded like the soft splutter of faraway gunfire.

From the belly of the Minerva the engines continued their rhythmic throbbing as the convict ship piloted its way through the blackness. Outside the porthole the stars twinkled, bright and cold, like light on diamond clusters. Estra had been swallowed up in the void. Somewhere ahead, light years away, planet Earth awaited Ailssa's return.

Ailssa stared at the photo, lost in her thoughts.

She saw the apology in Dante's eyes. She saw his strong back arching upwards and the balance and symmetry of his two broad shoulders as he tried to lift himself off the road with his arms. And she saw the tilt of his head and the tousled mop of brown hair which she had loved to touch.

She walked over to the telescreen and switched it off with one hand, at the same time dabbing a handkerchief at her single albino eye. Her third arm reached up to her cheek where she gently massaged the soft white fur which lay sleek and trim over her entire body.

Waking Up

———•◆━◆•◆•◆•——

Kate Stephens

"Do you have a pet theory, Mick?" said Warren. "I've never asked you before."

"About what, in particular?" I said.

"About the Sleep. What else?"

I looked in surprise at this neighbour and congenial pub companion of mine. On a superficial level I knew him well enough, but our conversations had never touched other than briefly on the subject of the Sleep before. I knew why: not even the most qualified experts could pretend that they had any answers, and Warren, being a doctor, shared the vast and silent embarrassment of the scientific community. Theories – yes, there were theories, but most of them tended towards the mystical and/or hysterical. Even at the highest levels, fear was the predominating factor. Russia blamed America and America blamed Russia and the rest of the world blamed both of them, but nobody was confident enough to start even a small war over it. Unbelievable it might be, but it had been the same everywhere. The aggressive nations shared their boat with mutual suspicion based on simple and complete bewilderment.

Nearly three months of this bewilderment had made it an extremely touchy subject between expert and layman. I knew that something must have agitated Warren for him to bring it up at all.

"Not really," I replied, after a moment's consideration. "Theorising seems a bit pointless."

"Pointless!" he barked. "The fact that there doesn't seem to be a reason only makes it more vital that we find one."

"You sound like you think you have," I observed.

He took a mouthful of his drink and shifted uncomfortably in his seat. "Call it a bad feeling."

"Bad feelings about the Sleep are ten a penny. It's hard to have any other kind. But if you look at it from a practical point of view, how much damage was done?"

He fairly pounced on that. "Exactly! What would you expect if the entire population of the world went into sudden and complete suspended animation?"

"Absolute chaos, I know. And I know there wasn't. It's been hashed and rehashed until everyone's sick of it. It just happened, and – "

I broke off, because he didn't seem to be listening. "It was so bloody orderly," he was saying. "People fell asleep in shifts. They just went to bed as usual and didn't wake up for a month. No industrial or shipping disasters. Not one power station failed or shut down. Everything kept running as smoothly as if there was still somebody in charge. There's really only one explanation for that."

I raised an eyebrow in encouragement, knowing what he was going to say because I'd heard it before, but not wishing to be rude.

"There must have been someone in charge," he went on. "Same thing exactly, here in Australia and over there in Russia, and everywhere in between. It's impossible to believe that there was no intelligence behind it. Someone wanted the human race out of action for a while, but didn't want to hurt it."

"So you don't subscribe to the Universal and Totally Harmless Virus theory," I said with a smirk.

"Don't bother trying to get a laugh," he growled. "It won't work. What most of us think and none of us say is that we were studied. Anaesthetised like laboratory rats and studied."

I didn't like his metaphor, but I nodded. "That's what most people are thinking."

"Right. Fine. But if you want to study a rat, you don't put every rat on the planet to sleep. I can't see that as being the real purpose behind it."

"Then you're talking experimental purposes."

"It might explain the kid gloves."

"But would it? If some other species wanted to run a few tests, it wouldn't matter if half the population died in the process. There'd still be enough left to show results. Anyway, it's a hell of a lot of trouble to go to when a cross-section would do just as well. Not to mention the fact that it's three months later and there's nothing to show that any such tests ever took place. You'd expect some sign of it by now."

He sighed heavily. Made a steeple of his fingers whilst chewing on his thumbnails, then, "But what if there is? Something that wasn't immediately obvious, but ... Anyway, 'experimental' is the wrong word."

"For what?" I prompted, beginning to take him seriously.

"I'm not the only one who's noticed," he said, voice lowering and eyes darting from side to side as if he expected to see a Thought Policeman lurking nearby. "And no one will talk about it."

"Well I'm talking about it," I said. "Or do you mean that no other doctor will?"

He blinked, shook his head to clear it. "I don't mean just the Sleep. I mean something else that every doctor must have noticed."

"What?" I said, now taking him very seriously.

"How may patients do you suppose I have who are expecting babies?" he asked, and I shrugged. "I should have about a dozen. Instead I have six. And they are all past their third month."

For a moment I could think of nothing to say. Warren appeared miserably pleased with the effect of his statement and merely waited.

"It couldn't be just a localised slump?" I said at length.

He shook his head, dabbling with purpose and a soggy coaster at a puddle of beer on the table. "That's the first possibility I checked. Or tried to. None of my colleagues, not even the ones I count as friends, none of them will say boo. They change the subject. They tell me not to jump to conclusions. But they can't deny that the only pregnant women around are three months or more."

"But what about the other areas, other countries?"

"The same, I'm willing to bet. A week ago I rang a friend in New York. He's an obstetrician. I asked how many expectant mothers he had on his books and he hung up. That's a fair answer."

"Are you saying it's worldwide?"

"Why not? The Sleep was."

"And are you saying it's connected?"

"Doesn't it follow? When I first noticed it, I thought it had to be some kind of trauma caused by the upset in the cycle – women didn't menstruate during the Sleep. But if so, it should have sorted itself out long ago."

"You can't say that for certain. Who can tell what effect a thing like that could have? There's no precedent."

"The menstrual cycle was back to normal in no time. The women are as healthy as usual. There's no medical reason I can see."

He fell silent, then rose abruptly and went to get himself another drink. He got me one as well, a kind of beer I loathe, but I said nothing and sipped it with good grace.

"You want to know what I think?" he said.

I nodded.

"It was planned that way. No, wait." He held up a hand, although I hadn't interrupted. "The rest was planned. Reasonable assumption?"

"I suppose so. It didn't have many random elements."

"Right. Then who planned it? I'd worked myself up a nice little theory, you know."

"Which is?"

"Well, there was the question of who'd be so concerned about the cost in human life. Answer – other humans. There's been a lot of interest in hibernation and suspended animation over the last few years. I didn't think the technology would be available to do it on a scale like that, but I'd allowed it as a possibility. But I still couldn't find a reason."

"And you think this could be the reason? To sterilise every woman on Earth? But why?"

"A last-ditch effort at birth control. In which case it wouldn't be every woman, and probably not permanent either. That's possible."

"Only just. The problem's not nearly critical enough to go that far. Parts of Asia, maybe, not Australia."

"You don't need to point out the holes in it. I know it's full of them. I don't really think it was some international ZPG program, and I don't think you'll find a single fertile woman anywhere. Or man, for that matter. Something as well organised as that wouldn't be taking chances."

"Something? So now you're talking aliens?"

A sharp, reluctant nod, and his hand curled unconsciously into a fist.

"But it still leaves the question," I said reasonably, "of why someone from Mars or Alpha Centauri would want to do that."

He gave me his best isn't-it-obvious-you-bloody-moron look and said, "What better way to clear a planet of human beings, if you're patient?"

"Hang on," I cautioned. "Aren't you jumping the gun a bit? This sterility, if it's as widespread as you think, could still be nothing more than a hangover from the Sleep."

He shook his head morosely. "No good. Animals – domesticated animals only, please note – went to Sleep too. My cat had a litter of kittens yesterday. Two months gestation."

"Maybe it's different for animals. A simpler brain ... "

The patient bleakness of his expression silenced me. It appeared he had more to impart.

"Mick," he said quietly, "the other day something happened that I think I'd better tell you about. I haven't told anyone else. I haven't been game."

"So tell," I said, wishing I knew what to expect.

Again the sideways flick of his gaze and the lowering of his voice as he began to speak.

"Sometime after lunch on Tuesday, a bloke I know quite well by sight came into the waiting room. Terry Camlann, his name is. He works for the solicitor next door to the surgery. Comes in now and again to pick up prescriptions for him."

He paused, as if he doubted the wisdom of continuing "Anyway, Camlann was chatting up my receptionist when a patient in the waiting room had an epileptic seizure. Camlann went to help him and was knocked flying. I came out to see what the noise was and found him out cold on the floor. The other man's fit had passed off in a few minutes, and he helped me carry Camlann into the surgery. I examined him; he was bleeding from a superficial head wound, but otherwise he seemed fine."

Warren hesitated again. I made an interrogative noise, and he took a deep breath. "It was his blood. It was too pale, too thin. I'd never seen anything like it, and all I could think of was that there had to be something terribly wrong with him. Then he woke up."

"And?"

"He was horrified to find himself in such a position. He seemed afraid. I asked if he was receiving medical attention and he said no, there was nothing wrong with him. He got up, even though he was shaky on his feet, and said he was very sorry for the inconvenience and he'd pay me for my trouble."

Warren frowned, as if at an irrelevance, and added, "Can you imagine that? Anyone else would've been ready to sue. Anyway, I tried to calm him down – he was still quite dizzy and disoriented. When the other patient had gone and we were alone, I told him he'd better see a doctor, and that if he wanted I'd examine him on the spot and refer him to a specialist."

"And what did he do?"

"I thought he was going to pass out again. He didn't even ask why I thought something was wrong with him. He just thanked me half a dozen times and said he was in a hurry. Then he went."

"And you let him go?" I said incredulously.

"What else could I do, short of restraining him by force? He's not my patient, anyway."

"I see. What happened then?"

"I couldn't stop thinking about him for the rest of the afternoon. As soon as my last patient had gone, I decided to have a closer look at that blood. There was plenty of it about – my handkerchief was covered in it. So I made up a slide and put it under a microscope."

He paused again. There was sweat on his forehead.

"Well?" I said. "What did you find?"

"It wasn't human blood at all," he said, looking at the table. "Terry Camlann isn't a human being. I don't see how he can be even distantly related to the human race. The cell structure was – bizarre. I can't even be sure it was a cell structure."

"There couldn't have been some mistake?" I said slowly.

"No. I went over every possibility. The blood under that microscope came from Terry Camlann, it wasn't mixed with anything else, and I can't see how it could have originated on this planet."

We both fell silent. The clink of glasses and the hum of after-work conversation from the bar came to us unnaturally loudly.

"Of course I went looking for him the next day – yesterday," Warren said eventually. "He wasn't at work. Or at home. All his belongings were gone. He'd done a bunk."

"Understandable," I allowed. "But who do you think he was?"

He gave me a crooked and unconvincing smile. "An observer," he replied simply. "One of Earth's future residents, taking notes on the soon-to-be-extinct species."

I swilled the rest of that obnoxious beer around in the glass and finished it with a shudder. "That doesn't necessarily follow, Warren."

He uttered a creaking laugh. "No, of course it doesn't. Sooner or later I'll come up with a perfectly simple explanation." He drained his glass "But in the meantime, let's have another, shall we?"

* * *

An hour later I left him to his drinking and went home, still thinking about what he'd told me. After dinner I was still so far away that Vicki had to ask three times whether I wanted a drink or not; I declined with a single shake of my head, and she came to sit beside me with a look in her eye that said my mood was undergoing thorough analysis.

"Oh, nothing really," I said, rather stupidly, in answer to her eventual query. "I heard a strange story in the pub this afternoon."

"One often hears strange stories in pubs," was her comment. "Particularly when one spends as much time in them as you do."

I smiled at her. In the five months since I'd replied to her advertisement for a flatmate she'd never voiced such an objection before, and I knew she was only doing it now to cover something else. I had noticed a certain abstraction and aloofness in her manner over the last week or so, and I knew I should be trying harder to discover the cause.

"Something on your mind?" I said.

"It can wait," she replied noncommittally. "What was the strange story you heard?"

I pondered for a moment, then said, "Imagine that you were someone from outer space who wanted to take over the Earth. How would you go about it?"

She gave every appearance of considering it seriously. "Terribly advanced of course? Way ahead of us, technology-wise?"

"You couldn't expect to get away with it with an M16 and a Volkswagen."

"With a view to dictatorship, or using the place to live on?"

"Using it to live on, I suppose."

"I'd sterilise every man, woman and child," she said, after thinking about it a bit more.

"You'd what?" I yelped.

"You heard. It'd be the logical thing to do. Killing everyone with weapons or poison would be messy and leave all the bodies to be cleared up. If one had the time and the patience – which you'd imagine more advanced beings to have – one could save a lot of trouble."

"But you – it –," I floundered, not knowing whether to tell her of Warren's fears. But I should have known what that common sense of hers was capable of.

"Was that the strange story you heard in the pub, Michael?" she said, with deceptive mildness.

I owned that it had been something along those lines.

"Don't look so amazed," she said. "It's not being supernaturally observant just to see what's right under your nose."

"Then you think that's why the Sleep happened too?"

"It's possible."

"It is ?" I said faintly.

"You forget that I work in an office block. There's 120 young women in that place, and at any given time ten of them are pregnant and fifty are trying to get that way. Right now, one is pregnant and fifty-nine are getting worried."

"Jesus," I said. "A doctor knocks his brains out wondering if it's just his extremist paranoia, and half his female patients could have told him all about it."

"Which doctor?" Vicki wanted to know. "What did he say?"

I told her. All of it.

"Well, well," she mused. "I didn't think it could've been just this corner of the world."

"But if you were suspicious, why didn't you tell anyone?"

Her pencil thin brows took an upward swoop. "Who'd pay attention?"

"But if the proof's right there?"

"You're missing the point. Who'd want to pay attention? I don't have facts and figures to back it up, never mind alien blood. Even if I did, people wouldn't want to listen. It'll make a sensational story in the paper when no one can ignore it any longer, but in the meantime nothing's going to be discussed or admitted publicly."

"You're talking as if it's a proven fact!"

"Yes I am, aren't I?"

"Well it isn't." The lack of conviction in my voice won a sour smile. "And even if it was, maybe whatever was done can be reversed. Cured. The reproductive system isn't much of a mystery these days."

"You've got a point, but don't you think that will have been allowed for? Whoever invented this game is in the best position to keep one step ahead. Of course, if there was no intelligence behind the Sleep at all and it was just a freak of nature, we've got nothing to worry about, have we?"

Further argument would sound hollow, and I knew it. A shrug might be misplaced, but it was all I had to offer.

"Maybe it's best to look at it philosophically, before the real panic starts," she went on with an unpleasant smile. "There have been a few gruesome threats hanging over the collective human head in the last forty years or so. We should be used to it. Besides, how does it affect me personally? I don't want kids. At worst, I'll live out my life and die decrepit, hoping there's some doddering old twit with enough wit left to bury me. No personal victims. Whoever's doing this isn't murdering us – only our posterity."

I couldn't answer her; I simply couldn't tell whether her indifference was assumed or real. "Do you think they really look like us?" was all I could find to say.

"They must," she answered. "That man – what was his name? Camlann. He's been passing as one of us for years."

"Maybe he was – well, in disguise," I suggested.

"He might have been. But they chose this planet out of God knows how many, and there must have been a reason for that. If there's an infinite number of worlds out there, who's to say that life on one of them – or more – couldn't evolve parallel to life on this one?"

"It could happen," I allowed.

"Yes. And if something went wrong there, they'd look for a planet just like it, and you can be sure they'd study it carefully. How much would it really surprise people to learn that there'd been aliens among us for generations, quietly studying? The idea isn't anything new."

"Neither's paranoia," I said gently.

She snorted. "I can't believe you're stupid enough to assume that because a thing is suspected and feared by a lot of people then it has to be mass hysteria. Anyway, I don't think it's unreasonable to suppose that if aliens were going to usurp this planet then they'd ensure that they had a complete record and analysis of its dominant life forms first."

"Would that be necessary?"

"It'd be common sense. I'd want to know a place and all its quirks properly, if it was me. Then there's their archives. They'd feel they owed it to us."

"Owed it? To us?" Vicki had me more than astonished now. She'd taken a hatful of hazy uncertainties and was pulling assumptions forth like tried and tested actualities.

"Yes," she said patiently, as if addressing a person of limited intelligence. "They're polite, if nothing else, and they have a genuine regard for life. They intend to take over, all right, but they're going about it in the kindest way they can."

"Vicki," I said uneasily, "all we know for sure is –"

"Oh, don't be such a pedant," she snapped. "Aren't I entitled to my wild imaginings? Anyway, a race as considerate as that would document mankind thoroughly while it was still around to be documented. Even we do that much for the species we're pushing out of existence."

"Okay," I said reluctantly. "So this is your scenario. A pack of aliens need the Earth to live on, so they remove the humans – who'd be bound to cause trouble – as gently as they can. They put research students all over the place because it's the least they can do. And we haven't even noticed them."

"I mean it hasn't made headlines. If they've been noticed, who'd listen? They're well trained, and they'll go to any lengths to blend in. Ordinary men in the street."

"Like Terry Camlann," I finished for her.

"Just like him. A front doesn't need to be elaborate to be convincing. A job, a home, maybe even a wife or husband. I wonder how you'd feel if you found out you'd been living with one of them. An alien, who was going to phase you out and replace you."

"I shrugged again, not liking the look in her eye. "It's not the kind of thing I ponder on daily."

"But what if it was a fact?" she pursued. All expression had suddenly gone from her face. If she'd only just walked in, I'd hardly have recognised her, she looked so different. And ... alien. It had never struck me before, but it struck me now.

"What if it was a fact, Michael? How would you feel?"

Some minutes ago I had begun to guess that I was being played with, but it shocked me to realise exactly what she had been leading up to all this time. She got to her feet.

She was standing over me now, and as I looked up at her I thought, "Her face is all wrong. The features are right, but not the finer expressions." So subtle as to be barely perceptible, but still the lack was there.

I didn't need to answer. I didn't need to tell her how I'd feel. All I could force my mouth to say was, "Why are you so sure?"

Her reply was simple. One of the risks we had overlooked.

"You answer questions," she said, "when you talk in your sleep."

Then she picked up the nearest thing to hand – it was a dictionary from the coffee table – and flung it at me. It struck my forehead, and a dozen tiny stars blazed momentarily across my field of vision; when I put up my hand, it came away wet with blood. Not much, but still she could see its colour.

There was a moment's oppressive silence, then she turned on her heel and walked out.

I drew a deep breath and let it out shakily, thinking how glad I'd be to get home. They have no manners here.

Nothing To Be Afraid Of

Jan Mark

"Robin won't give you any trouble," said Auntie Lynn. "He's very quiet."

Anthea knew how quiet Robin was. At present he was sitting under the table and, until Auntie Lynn mentioned his name, she had forgotten that he was there.

Auntie Lynn put a carrier bag on the armchair.

"There's plenty of clothes, so you won't need to do any washing, and there's a spare pair of pyjamas in case – well, you know. In case..."

"Yes," said Mum, firmly. "He'll be all right. I'll ring you tonight and let you know how he's getting along." She looked at the clock. "Now, hadn't you better be getting along?"

She saw Auntie Lynn to the front door and Anthea heard them saying good-bye to each other. Mum almost told Auntie Lynn to stop worrying and have a good time, which would have been a mistake because Auntie Lynn was going up North to a funeral.

Auntie Lynn was not really an Aunt, but she had once been at school with Anthea's mum, and she was the kind of person who couldn't manage without a handle to her name; so Robin was not Anthea's cousin. Robin was not anything much, except four years old, and he looked a lot younger; probably because nothing ever happened to him. Auntie Lynn kept no pets that might give Robin germs, and never bought him toys that had sharp corners to dent him or wheels that could be swallowed. He wore balaclava helmets and bobble hats in winter to protect his tender ears, and a knitted vest under his shirt in summer in case he overheated himself and caught a chill from his own sweat.

"Perspiration," said Auntie Lynn.

His face was as pale and flat as a saucer of milk, and his eyes floated in it like drops of cod-liver oil. This was not surprising as he was full to the back teeth with cod-liver oil; also with extract of malt, concentrated orange juice and calves-foot jelly. When you picked him up you expected him to squelch, like a hot-water bottle full of half-set custard.

Anthea lifted the tablecloth and looked at him.

"Hello, Robin."

Robin stared at her with his flat eyes and went back to sucking his woolly doggy that had flat eyes also, of sewn-on felt, because glass ones might find their way into Robin's appendix and cause damage. Anthea wondered how long it would be before he noticed that his mother had gone. Probably he wouldn't, any more than he would notice when she came back.

Mum closed the front door and joined Anthea in looking under the table at Robin. Robin's mouth turned down at the corners, and Anthea hoped he would cry so that they could cuddle him. It seemed impolite to cuddle him before he needed it. Anthea was afraid to go any closer.

"What a little troll," said Mum, sadly, lowering the tablecloth. "I suppose he'll come out when he's hungry."

Anthea doubted it.

Robin didn't want any lunch or any tea.

"Do you think he's pining?" said Mum. Anthea did not. Anthea had a nasty suspicion that he was like this all the time. He went to bed without making a fuss and fell asleep before the light was out, as if he were too bored to stay awake. Anthea left her bedroom door open, hoping that he would have a nightmare so that she could go in and comfort him, but Robin slept all night without a squeak, and woke in the morning as flat-faced as before. Wall-eyed Doggy looked more excitable than Robin did.

"If only we had a proper garden," said Mum, as Robin went under the table again, leaving his breakfast eggs scattered round the plate. "He might run about."

Anthea thought that this was unlikely, and in any case they didn't have a proper garden, only a yard at the back and a stony strip in front, without a fence.

"Can I take him to the park?" said Anthea.

Mum looked doubtful. "Do you think he wants to go?"

"No," said Anthea, peering under the tablecloth. "I don't think he wants to do anything, but he can't sit there all day."

"I bet he can," said Mum. "Still, I don't think he should. All right, take him to the park, but keep quiet about it. I don't suppose Lynn thinks you're safe in traffic."

"He might tell her."

"Can he talk?"

Robin, still clutching wall-eyed Doggy, plodded beside her all the way to the park, without once trying to jam his head between the library railings or get run over by a bus.

"Hold my hand, Robin," Anthea said as they left the house, and he clung to her like a lamprey.

The park was not really a park at all; it was a garden. It did not even pretend to be a park and the notice by the gate said KING STREET GARDENS, in case anyone tried to use it as a park. The grass was as green and as flat as the front-room carpet, but the front-room carpet had a path worn across it from the door to the fireplace, and here there were more notices that said KEEP OFF THE GRASS, so that the gritty white paths went obediently round the edge, under the orderly trees that stood in a row like the queue outside a fish shop. There were bushes in each corner and one shelter with a bench in it. Here and there brown holes in the grass, full of raked earth, waited for next year's flowers, but there were no flowers now, and the bench had been taken out of the shelter because the shelter was supposed to be a summer-house, and you couldn't have people using a summer-house in winter.

Robin stood by the gates and gaped, with Doggy depending limply from his mouth where he held it by one ear, between his teeth. Anthea decided that if they met anyone she knew, she would explain that Robin was only two, but very big for his age.

"Do you want to run, Robin?"

Robin shook his head.

"There's nothing to be afraid of. You can go all the way round, if you like, but you mustn't walk on the grass or pick things."

Robin nodded. It was the kind of place that he understood.

Anthea sighed. "Well, let's walk round, then."

They set off. At each corner, where the bushes were, the path diverged. One part went in front of the bushes, one part round the back of them. On the first circuit Robin stumped glumly beside Anthea in front of the bushes. The second time round she felt a very faint tug at her hand. Robin wanted to go his own way.

This called for a celebration. Robin could think. Anthea crouched down on the path until they were at the same level.

"You want to walk round the back of the bushes, Robin?"

"Yiss," said Robin.

Robin could *talk*.

"All right, but listen." She lowered her voice to a whisper. "You must be very careful. That path is called Leopard Walk. Do you know what a leopard is?"

"Yiss."

"There are two leopards down there. They live in the bushes. One is a good leopard and the other's a bad leopard. The good leopard has black spots. The bad leopard has red spots. If you see the bad leopard you must say, 'Die leopard die or I'll kick you in the eye', and run like anything. Do you understand?"

Robin tugged again.

"Oh no," said Anthea. "I'm going *this* way. If you want to go down Leopard Walk, you'll have to go on your own. I'll meet you at the other end. Remember, if it's got red spots, run like mad."

Robin trotted away. The bushes were just high enough to hide him, but Anthea could see the bobble on his hat doddering along. Suddenly the bobble gathered speed and Anthea had to run to reach the end of the bushes first.

"Did you see the bad leopard?"

"No," said Robin, but he didn't look too sure.

"Why were you running, then?"

"I just wanted to."

"You've dropped Doggy," said Anthea. Doggy lay on the path with his legs in the air, halfway down Leopard Walk.

"You get him," said Robin.

"No, you get him," said Anthea. "I'll wait here." Robin moved off, reluctantly. She waited until he had recovered Doggy and then shouted, "I can see the bad leopard in the bushes!" Robin raced back to safety. "Did you say, 'Die leopard die or I'll kick you in the eye'?" Anthea demanded.

"No," Robin said, guiltily.

"Then he'll *kill* us," said Anthea. "Come on, run. We've got to get to that tree. He can't hurt us once we're under that tree."

They stopped running under the twisted boughs of a weeping ash. "This is a python tree," said Anthea. "Look, you can see the python wound round the trunk."

"What's a python?" asked Robin, backing off.

"Oh, it's just a great big snake that squeezes people to death," said Anthea. "A python could easily eat a leopard. That's why leopards won't walk under this tree, you see, Robin."

Robin looked up. "Could it eat us?"

"Yes, but it won't if we walk on our heels." They walked on their heels to the next corner.

"Are there leopards down there?"

"No, but we must never go down there anyway. That's Poison Alley. All the trees are poisonous. They drip poison. If one bit of poison fell on your head, you'd die."

"I've got my hat on," said Robin, touching the bobble to make sure.

"It would burn right through your hat," Anthea assured him. "Right into your brains. *Fzzzzzzz.*"

They bypassed Poison Alley and walked on over the manhole cover that clanked.

"What's that?"

"That's the Fever Pit. If anyone lifts that manhole cover, they get a terrible disease. There's this terrible disease down there, Robin, and if the lid comes off, the disease will get out and people will die. I should think there's enough disease down there to kill everybody in this town. It's ever so loose, look."

"Don't lift it! Don't lift it!" Robin screamed, and ran to the shelter for safety.

"Don't go in there," yelled Anthea. "That's where the Greasy Witch lives." Robin bounced out of the shelter as though he were on elastic.

"Where's the Greasy Witch?"

"Oh, you can't see her," said Anthea, "but you can tell where she is because she smells so horrible. I think she must be somewhere about. Can't you smell her now?"

Robin sniffed the air and clasped Doggy more tightly.

"And she leaves oily marks wherever she goes. Look, you can see them on the wall."

Robin looked at the wall. Someone had been very busy, if not the Greasy Witch. Anthea was glad on the whole that Robin could not read.

"The smell's getting worse, isn't it, Robin? I think we'd better go down here and then she won't find us."

"She'll see us."

"No, she won't. She can't see with her eyes because they're full of grease. She sees with her ears, but I expect they're all waxy. She's a filthy old witch, really."

They slipped down a secret-looking path that went round the back of the shelter.

"Is the Greasy Witch down here?" said Robin, fearfully.

"I don't know," said Anthea. "Let's investigate." They tiptoed round the side of the shelter. The path was damp and slippery. "Filthy old witch. She's certainly been here," said Anthea. "I think she's gone now. I'll just have a look."

She craned her neck round the corner of the shelter. There was a sort of glade in the bushes, and in the middle was a stand-pipe, with a tap on top. The pipe was lagged with canvas, like a scaly skin.

"Frightful Corner," said Anthea. Robin put his cautious head round the edge of the shelter.

"What's that?"

Anthea wondered if it could be a dragon, up on the tip of its tail and ready to strike, but on the other side of the bushes was the brick back wall of the King Street Public Conveniences, and at that moment she heard the unmistakable sound of a cistern flushing.

"It's a Lavatory Demon," she said. "Quick! We've got to get away before the water stops, or he'll have us."

They ran all the way to the gates, where they could see the church clock, and it was almost time for lunch.

Auntie Lynn fetched Robin home next morning, and three days later she was back again, striding up the path like a warrior queen going into battle, with Robin dangling from her hand, and Doggy dangling from Robin's hand.

Mum took her into the front room, closing the door. Anthea sat on the stairs and listened. Auntie Lynn was in full throat and furious, so it was easy enough to hear what she had to say.

"I want a word with that young lady," said Auntie Lynn. "And I want to know what she's been telling him." Her voice dropped, and Anthea could hear only certain fateful words: "Leopards...poison trees...snakes... diseases!"

Mum said something very quietly that Anthea did not hear, and then Auntie Lynn turned up the volume once more.

"Won't go to bed unless I leave the door open ... wants the light on ... up and down to him all night ... won't go to the bathroom on his own. He says the-the-," she hesitated, "the toilet demons will get him. He nearly broke his neck running downstairs this morning."

Mum spoke again, but Auntie Lynn cut in like a band-saw.

"Frightened out of his wits! He follows me everywhere."

The door opened slightly, and Anthea got ready to bolt, but it was Robin who came out, with his thumb in his mouth and circles round his eyes. Under his arm was soggy Doggy, ears chewed to nervous rags.

Robin looked up at Anthea through the bannisters.

"Let's go to the park," he said.

The Open Window

'Saki' (H. H. Munro)

"My aunt will be down presently, Mr Nuttel," said a very self-possessed young lady of fifteen; "in the meantime you must try and put up with me."

Framton Nuttel endeavoured to say the correct something which should duly flatter the niece of the moment without unduly discounting the aunt that was to come. Privately he doubted more than ever whether these formal visits on a succession of total strangers would do much towards helping the nerve cure which he was supposed to be undergoing.

"I know how it will be," his sister had said when he was preparing to migrate to this rural retreat; "you will bury yourself down there and not speak to a living soul, and your nerves will be worse than ever from moping. I shall just give you letters of introduction to all the people I know there. Some of them, as far as I can remember, were quite nice."

Framton wondered whether Mrs Sappleton, the lady to whom he was presenting one of the letters of introduction, came into the nice division.

"Do you know many of the people round here?" asked the niece, when she judged that they had had sufficient silent communion.

"Hardly a soul," said Framton. "My sister was staying here, at the rectory, you know, some four years ago, and she gave me letters of introduction to some of the people here."

He made the last statement in a tone of distinct regret.

"Then you know practically nothing about my aunt?" pursued the self-possessed young lady.

"Only her name and address," admitted the caller. He was wondering whether Mrs Sappleton was in the married or widowed state. An undefinable something about the room seemed to suggest masculine habitation.

"Her great tragedy happened just three years ago," said the child; "that would be since your sister's time."

"Her tragedy?" asked Framton; somehow in this restful country spot tragedies seemed out of place.

"You may wonder why we keep that window wide open on an October afternoon," said the niece, indicating a large French window that opened on to a lawn.

"It is quite warm for the time of the year," said Framton; "but has that window got anything to do with the tragedy?"

"Out through that window, three years ago to a day, her husband and her two young brothers went off for their day's shooting. They never came back. In crossing the moor to their favourite snipe-shooting ground they were all three engulfed in a treacherous piece of bog. It had been that dreadful wet summer, you know, and places that were safe in other years gave way suddenly without warning. Their bodies were never recovered. That was the dreadful part of it." Here the child's voice lost its self-possessed note and became falteringly human. "Poor aunt always thinks that they will come back some day, they and the little brown spaniel that was lost with them, and walk in at that window just as they used to do. That is why the window is kept open every evening till it is quite dusk. Poor dear aunt, she has often told me how they went out, her husband with his white waterproof coat over his arm, and Ronnie, her youngest brother, singing, 'Bertie, why do you bound?' as he always did to tease her, because she said it got on her nerves. Do you know, sometimes on still, quiet evenings like this, I almost get a creepy feeling that they will all walk in through that window –"

She broke off with a little shudder. It was a relief to Framton when the aunt bustled into the room with a whirl of apologies for being late in making her appearance.

"I hope Vera has been amusing you?" she said.

"She has been very interesting," said Framton.

"I hope you don't mind the open window," said Mrs Sappleton briskly; "my husband and brothers will be home directly from shooting, and they always come in this way. They've been out for snipe in the marshes today, so they'll make a fine mess over my poor carpets. So like you men-folk, isn't it?"

She rattled on cheerfully about the shooting and the scarcity of birds, and the prospects for duck in the winter. To Framton it was all purely horrible. He made a desperate but only partially successful effort to turn the talk on to a less ghastly topic; he was conscious that his hostess was giving him only a fragment of her attention, and her eyes were constantly straying past him to the open window and the lawn beyond. It was certainly an unfortunate coincidence that he should have paid his visit on this tragic anniversary.

"The doctors agree in ordering me complete rest, an absence of mental excitement, and avoidance of anything in the nature of violent physical exercise," announced Framton, who laboured under the tolerably widespread delusion that total strangers and chance acquaintances are hungry for the least detail of one's ailments and infirmities, their cause and cure. "On the matter of diet they are not so much in agreement," he continued.

"No?" said Mrs Sappleton, in a voice which only replaced a yawn at the last moment. Then she suddenly brightened into alert attention – but not to what Framton was saying.

"Here they are at last!" she cried. "Just in time for tea, and don't they look as if they were muddy up to the eyes!"

Framton shivered slightly and turned towards the niece with a look intended to convey sympathetic comprehension. The child was staring out through the open window with dazed horror in her eyes. In a chill shock of nameless fear Framton swung round in his seat and looked in the same direction.

In the deepening twilight three figures were walking across the lawn towards the window; they all carried guns under their arms, and one of them was additionally burdened with a white coat hung over his shoulders. A tired brown spaniel kept close at their heels. Noiselessly they neared the house, and then a hoarse young voice chanted out of the dusk: "I said, Bertie, why do you bound?"

Framton grabbed wildly at his stick and hat; the hall-door, the gravel-drive, and the front gate were dimly noted stages in his headlong retreat. A cyclist coming along the road had to run into the hedge to avoid imminent collision.

"Here we are, my dear," said the bearer of the white mackintosh, coming in through the window; "fairly muddy, but most of it's dry. Who was that who bolted out as we came up?"

"A most extraordinary man, a Mr Nuttel," said Mrs Sappleton; "could only talk about his illnesses, and dashed off without a word of good-bye or apology when you arrived. One would think he had seen a ghost."

"I expect it was the spaniel," said the niece calmly; "he told me he had a horror of dogs. He was once hunted into a cemetery somewhere on the banks of the Ganges by a pack of pariah dogs, and had to spend the night in a newly dug grave with the creatures snarling and grinning and foaming just above him. Enough to make anyone lose their nerve."

Romance at short notice was her speciality.

The Tell-Tale Heart

Edgar Allan Poe

True! – nervous – very, very dreadfully nervous I had been and am; but why *will* you say that I am mad? The disease had sharpened my senses – not destroyed – not dulled them. Above all was the sense of hearing acute. I heard all things in the heaven and in the earth. I heard many things in hell. How, then, am I mad? Hearken! and observe how healthily – how calmly I can tell you the whole story.

It is impossible to say how first the idea entered my brain; but once conceived, it haunted me day and night. Object there was none. Passion there was none. I loved the old man. He had never wronged me. He had never given me insult. For his gold I had no desire. I think it was his eye! Yes, it was this! One of his eyes resembled that of a vulture – a pale blue eye, with a film over it. Whenever it fell upon me, my blood ran cold; and so by degrees – very gradually – I made up my mind to take the life of the old man, and thus rid myself of the eye for ever.

Now this is the point. You fancy me mad. Madmen know nothing. But you should have seen *me*. You should have seen how wisely I proceeded – with what caution – with what foresight – with what dissimulation I went to work! I was never kinder to the old man than during the whole week before I killed him. And every night, about midnight, I turned the latch of his door and opened it – oh, so gently! And then, when I had made an opening sufficient for my head, I put in a dark lantern, all closed, closed, so that no light shone out, and then I thrust in my head. Oh, you would have laughed to see how cunningly I thrust it in! I moved it slowly – very, very slowly, so that I might not disturb the old man's sleep. It took me an hour to place my whole head within the opening so far that I could see him as he lay upon his bed. Ha! – would a madman have been so wise as this? And then, when my head was well in the room, I undid the lantern cautiously – oh, so cautiously – cautiously (for the hinges creaked) – I undid it just so much that a single thin ray fell upon the vulture eye. And this I did for seven long nights – every night just at midnight – but I found the eye always closed; and so it was impossible to do the work; for it was not the old man who vexed me, but his Evil Eye. And every morning, when the day broke, I went boldly into the chamber, and spoke courageously to him, calling him by name in a hearty tone, and inquiring how he had passed the night. So you see he would have been a very profound old man, indeed, to suspect that every night, just at twelve, I looked in upon him while he slept.

Upon the eighth night I was more than usually cautious in opening the door. A watch's minute hand moves more quickly than did mine. Never before that night had I *felt* the extent of my own powers – of my sagacity. I could scarcely contain my feelings of triumph. To think that there I was, opening the door, little by little, and he not even to dream of my secret deeds or thoughts. I fairly chuckled at the idea; and perhaps he heard me; for he moved on the bed suddenly, as if startled. Now you may think that I drew back – but no. His room was as black as pitch with the thick darkness (for the shutters were close fastened, through fear of robbers), and so I knew that he could not see the opening of the door, and I kept pushing it on steadily, steadily.

I had my head in, and was about to open the lantern, when my thumb slipped upon the tin fastening, and the old man sprang up in the bed, crying out – "Who's there?"

I kept quite still and said nothing. For a whole hour I did not move a muscle, and in the meantime I did not hear him lie down.

He was still sitting up in the bed listening; – just as I have done, night after night, hearkening to the death watches in the wall.

Presently I heard a slight groan, and I knew it was the groan of mortal terror. It was not a groan of pain or of grief – oh, no! – it was the low stifled sound that arises from the bottom of the soul when overcharged with awe. I knew the sound well. Many a night, just at midnight, when all the world slept, it has welled up from my own bosom, deepening, with its dreadful echo, the terrors that distracted me. I say I knew it well. I knew what the old man felt, and pitied him, although I chuckled at heart. I knew that he had been lying awake ever since the first slight noise, when he had turned in the bed. His fears had been ever since growing upon him. He had been trying to fancy them causeless, but could not. He had been saying to himself – "It is nothing but the wind in the chimney – it is only a mouse crossing the floor," or "it is merely a cricket which has made a single chirp." Yes, he has been trying to comfort himself with these suppositions; but he had found all in vain. *All in vain;* because Death, in approaching him, had stalked with his black shadow before him, and enveloped the victim. And it was the mournful influence of the unperceived shadow that caused him to feel – although he neither saw nor heard – to *feel* the presence of my head within the room.

When I had waited a long time, very patiently, without hearing him lie down, I resolved to open a little – a very, very little crevice in the lantern. So I opened it – you cannot imagine how stealthily, stealthily – until, at length, a single dim ray, like the thread of the spider, shot from out the crevice and full upon the vulture eye.

It was open – wide, wide open – and I grew furious as I gazed upon it. I saw it with perfect distinctness – all a dull blue, with a hideous veil over it that chilled the very marrow in my bones; but I could see nothing else of the old man's face or person: for I had directed the ray as if by instinct, precisely upon the damned spot.

And now have I not told you that what you mistake for madness is but over-acuteness of the senses? – now, I say, there came to my ears a low, dull, quick sound, such as a watch makes when enveloped in cotton. I knew *that* sound well too. It was the beating of the old man's heart. It increased my fury, as the beating of a drum stimulates the soldier into courage.

But even yet I refrained and kept still. I scarcely breathed. I held the lantern motionless. I tried how steadily I could maintain the ray upon the eye. Meantime the hellish tattoo of the heart increased. It grew quicker and quicker, and louder and louder every instant. The old man's terror *must* have been extreme! It grew louder, I say, louder every moment! – do you mark me well? I have told you that I am nervous: so I am. And now at the dead hour of the night, amid the dreadful silence of that old house, so strange a noise as this excited me to uncontrollable terror. Yet, for some minutes longer I refrained and stood still. But the beating grew louder, louder! I thought the heart must burst. And now a new anxiety seized me – the sound would be heard by a neighbour! The old man's hour had come! With a loud yell, I threw open the lantern and leaped into the room. He shrieked once – once only. In an instant I dragged him to the floor, and pulled the heavy bed over him. I then smiled gaily, to find the deed so far done. But, for many minutes, the heart beat on with a muffled sound. This, however, did not vex me; it would not be heard through the wall. At length it ceased. The old man was dead. I removed the bed and examined the corpse. Yes, he was stone, stone dead. I placed my hand upon the heart and held it there many minutes. There was no pulsation. He was stone dead. His eye would trouble me no more.

If still you think me mad, you will think so no longer when I describe the wise precautions I took for the concealment of the body. The night waned, and I worked hastily, but in silence. First of all I dismembered the corpse. I cut off the head and the arms and the legs.

I then took up three planks from the flooring of the chamber, and deposited all between the scantlings. I then replaced the boards so cleverly, so cunningly, that no human eye – not even *his* – could have detected anything wrong. There was nothing to wash out – no stain of any kind – no blood spot whatever. I had been too wary for that. A tub had caught all – ha! ha!

When I had made an end of these labours, it was four o'clock – still dark as midnight. As the bell sounded the hour, there came a knocking at the street door. I went down to open it with a light heart, – for what had I *now* to fear? There entered three men, who introduced themselves, with perfect suavity, as officers of the police. A shriek had been heard by a neighbour during the night; suspicion of foul play had been aroused; information had been lodged at the police office, and they (the officers) had been deputed to search the premises.

I smiled, – for *what* had I to fear? I bade the gentlemen welcome. The shriek, I said, was my own in a dream. The old man, I mentioned, was absent in the country. I took my visitors all over the house. I bade them search – search *well*. I led them, at length, to *his* chamber. I showed them his treasures, secure, undisturbed. In the enthusiasm of my confidence, I brought chairs into the room, and desired them *here* to rest from their fatigues, while I myself, in the wild audacity of my perfect triumph, placed my own seat upon the very spot beneath which reposed the corpse of the victim.

The officers were satisfied. My *manner* had convinced them. I was singularly at ease. They sat, and while I answered cheerily, they chatted familiar things. But, ere long, I felt myself getting pale and wished them gone. My head ached, and I fancied a ringing in my ears: but still they sat and still they chatted. The ringing became more distinct: – it continued and became more distinct: I talked more freely to get rid of the feeling: but it continued and gained definitiveness – until, at length, I found that the noise was *not* within my ears.

No doubt I now grew *very* pale; – but I talked more fluently, and with a heightened voice. Yet the sound increased – and what could I do? It was *a low, dull, quick sound - much such a sound as a watch makes when enveloped in cotton.* I gasped for breath – and yet the officers heard it not. I talked more quickly – more vehemently; but the noise steadily increased. I arose and argued about trifles, in a high key and with violent gesticulations, but the noise steadily increased. Why *would* they not be gone? I paced the floor to and fro with heavy strides, as if excited to fury by the observation of the men – but the noise steadily increased. Oh God! what *could* I do? I foamed – I raved – I swore! I swung the chair upon which I had been sitting, and grated it upon the boards, but the noise arose over all and continually increased. It grew louder – louder – *louder*! And still the men chatted pleasantly, and smiled. Was it possible they heard not? Almighty God! – no, no! They heard! – they suspected! – they *knew*! – they were making a mockery of my horror! – this I thought, and this I think. But anything was better than this agony! Anything was more tolerable than this derision! I could bear those hypocritical smiles no longer! I felt that I must scream or die! – and now – again! – hark! louder! louder! louder! *louder*! –

"Villains!" I shrieked, "dissemble no more! I admit the deed! – tear up the planks! – here, here! – it is the beating of his hideous heart!"

The Second Bullet

Anna Katharine Green

—————•◆◆◆•—————

" You must see her."

"No. No."

"She's a most unhappy woman. Husband and child both taken from her in a moment; and now, all means of living as well, unless some happy thought of yours – some inspiration of your genius – shows us a way of re-establishing her claims to the policy voided by this cry of suicide."

But the small wise head of Violet Strange continued its slow shake of decided refusal.

"I'm sorry;" she protested, "but it's quite out of my province. I'm too young to meddle with so serious a matter."

"Not when you can save a bereaved woman the only possible compensation left her by untoward fate?"

"Let the police try their hand at that."

"They have had no success with the case."

"Or you?"

"Nor I either."

"And you expect –"

"Yes, Miss Strange. I expect you to find the missing bullet which will settle the fact that murder and not suicide ended George Hammond's life. If you cannot, then a long litigation awaits this poor widow, ending, as such litigation usually does, in favour of the stronger party. There's the alternative. If you once saw her –"

"But that's what I'm not willing to do. If I once saw her I should yield to her importunities and attempt the seemingly impossible. My instincts bid me say no. Give me something easier."

"Easier things are not so remunerative. There's money in this affair, if the insurance company is forced to pay up. I can offer you –"

"What?"

There was eagerness in the tone despite her effort at nonchalance. The other smiled imperceptibly, and briefly named the sum.

It was larger than she had expected. This her visitor saw by the way her eyelids fell and the peculiar stillness which, for an instant, held her vivacity in check.

"And you think I can earn that?"

Her eyes were fixed on his in an eagerness as honest as it was unrestrained.

He could hardly conceal his amazement, her desire was so evident and the cause of it so difficult to understand. He knew she wanted money – that was her avowed reason for entering into this uncongenial work. But to want it so *much*! He glanced at her person; it was simply clad but very expensively – how expensively it was his business to know. Then he took in the room in which they sat. Simplicity again, but the simplicity of high art – the drawing-room of one rich enough to indulge in the final luxury of a highly cultivated taste, viz: unostentatious elegance and the subjection of each carefully chosen ornament to the general effect.

What did this favoured child of fortune lack that she could be reached by such a plea, when her whole being revolted from the nature of the task he offered her? It was a question not new to him; but one he had never heard answered and was not likely to hear answered now. But the fact remained that the consent he had thought dependent upon sympathetic interest could be reached much more readily by the promise of large emolument – and he owned to a feeling of secret disappointment even while he recognised the value of the discovery.

But his satisfaction in the latter, if satisfaction it were, was of very short duration. Almost immediately he observed a change in her. The sparkle which had shone in the eye whose depths he had never been able to penetrate, had dissipated itself in something like a tear and she spoke up in that vigorous tone no one but himself had ever heard, as she said:

"No. The sum is a good one and 1 could use it; but 1 will not waste my energy on a case I do not believe in. The man shot himself He was a speculator, and probably had good reason for his act. Even his wife acknowledges that he has lately had more losses than gains."

"See her. She has something to tell you which never got into the papers."

"You say that? You know that?"

"On my honour, Miss Strange."

Violet pondered; then suddenly succumbed.

"Let her come, then. Prompt to the hour. I will receive her at three. Later I have a tea and two party calls to make."

Her visitor rose to leave. He had been able to subdue all evidence of his extreme gratification, and now took on a formal air. In dismissing a guest, Miss Strange was invariably the society belle and that only. This he had come to recognise.

The case (well known at the time) was, in the fewest possible words, as follows:

On a sultry night in September, a young couple living in one of the large apartment houses in the extreme upper portion of Manhattan were so annoyed by the incessant crying of a child in the adjoining suite, that they got up, he to smoke, and she to sit in the window for a possible breath of cool air. They were congratulating themselves upon the wisdom they had shown in thus giving up all thought of sleep – for the child's crying had not ceased – when (it may have been two o'clock and it may have been a little later) there came from somewhere near, the sharp and somewhat peculiar detonation of a pistol-shot.

He thought it came from above; she, from the rear, and they were staring at each other in the helpless wonder of the moment, when they were struck by the silence. The baby had ceased to cry. All was as still in the adjoining apartment as in their own – too still – much too still Their mutual stare turned to one of horror. "It came from there!" whispered the wife. "Some accident has occurred to Mr or Mrs Hammond – we ought to go –"

Her words – very tremulous ones – were broken by a shout from below. They were standing in their window and had evidently been seen by a passing policeman. "Anything wrong up there?" they heard him cry. Mr Saunders immediately looked out. "Nothing wrong here," he called down. (They were but two storeys from the pavement.) "But I'm not so sure about the rear apartment. We thought we heard a shot. Hadn't you better come up, officer? My wife is nervous about it. I'll meet you at the stair-head and show you the way."

The officer nodded and stepped in. The young couple hastily donned some wraps, and, by the time he appeared on their floor, they were ready to accompany him.

Meanwhile, no disturbance was apparent anywhere else in the house, until the policeman rang the bell of the Hammond apartment. Then, voices began to be heard, and doors to open above and below, but not the one before which the policeman stood.

Another ring, and this time an insistent one; and still no response. The officer's hand was rising for the third time when there came a sound of fluttering from behind the panels against which he had laid his ear, and finally a choked voice uttering unintelligible words. Then a hand began to struggle with the lock, and the door, slowly opening, disclosed a woman clad in a hastily donned wrapper and giving every evidence of extreme fright.

"Oh!" she exclaimed, seeing only the compassionate faces of her neighbours. "You heard it, too! A pistol-shot from there – *there* my husband's room. I have not dared to go – I – I – O, have mercy and see if anything is wrong! It is so still – so still, and only a moment ago the baby was crying. Mrs Saunders, Mrs Saunders, why is it so still?"

She had fallen into her neighbour's arms. The hand with which she had pointed out a certain door had sunk to her side and she appeared to be on the verge of collapse.

The officer eyed her sternly, while noting her appearance, which was that of a woman hastily risen from bed.

"Where were you?" he asked. "Not with your husband and child, or you would know what had happened there."

"I was sleeping down the hall," she managed to gasp out. "I'm not well – I – Oh, why do you all stand still and do nothing? My baby's in there. Go! go!" and, with a sudden energy, she sprang upright, her eyes wide open and burning, her small well-featured face white as the linen she sought to hide.

The officer demurred no longer. In another instant he was trying the door at which she was again pointing.

It was locked.

Glancing back at the woman, now cowering almost to the floor, he pounded at the door and asked the man inside to open.

No answer came back.

With a sharp turn he glanced again at the wife.

"You say that your husband is in this room?"

She nodded, gasping faintly, "And the child!"

He turned back, listened, then beckoned to Mr Saunders. "We shall have to break our way in," said he. "Put your shoulder well to the door. Now!"

The hinges of the door creaked; the lock gave way (this special officer weighed two hundred and seventy-five, as he found out, next day), and a prolonged and sweeping crash told the rest.

Mrs Hammond gave a low cry; and, straining forward from where she crouched in terror on the floor, searched the faces of the two men for some hint of what they saw in the dimly-lighted space beyond.

Something dreadful, something which made Mr Saunders come rushing back with a shout:

"Take her away! Take her to our apartment, Jennie. She must not see – ."

Not see! He realised the futility of his words as his gaze fell on the young woman who had risen up at his approach and now stood gazing at him without speech, without movement, but with a glare of terror in her eyes, which gave him his first realisation of human misery.

His own glance fell before it. If he had followed his instinct he would have fled the house rather than answer the question of her look and the attitude of her whole frozen body.

Perhaps in mercy to his speechless terror, perhaps in mercy to herself, she was the one who at last found the word which voiced their mutual anguish.

"Dead?"

No answer. None was needed.

"And my baby?"

O, that cry! It curdled the hearts of all who heard it. It shook the souls of men and women both inside and outside the apartment; then all was forgotten in the wild rush she made. The wife and mother had flung herself upon the scene, and, side by side with the not unmoved policeman, stood looking down upon the desolation made in one fatal instant in her home and heart.

They lay there together, both past help, both quite dead. The child had simply been strangled by the weight of his father's arm which lay directly across the upturned little throat. But the father was a victim of the shot they had heard. There was blood on his breast, and a pistol in his hand.

Suicide! The horrible truth was patent. No wonder they wanted to hold the young widow back. Her neighbour, Mrs Saunders, crept in on tiptoe and put her arms about the swaying, fainting woman; but there was nothing to say – absolutely nothing.

At least, they thought not. But when they saw her throw herself down, not by her husband, but by the child, and drag it out from under that strangling arm and hug and kiss it and call out wildly for a doctor, the officer endeavoured to interfere and yet could not find the heart to do so, though he knew the child was dead and should not, according to all the rules of the coroner's office, be moved before that official arrived. Yet because no mother could be convinced of a fact like this, he let her sit with it on the floor and try all her little arts to revive it, while he gave orders to the janitor and waited himself for the arrival of doctor and coroner.

She was still sitting there in wide-eyed misery, alternately fondling the little body and drawing back to consult its small set features for some sign of life, when the doctor came, and, after one look at the child, drew it softly from her arms and laid it quietly in the crib from which its father had evidently lifted it but a short time before. Then he turned back to her, and found her on her feet, upheld by her two friends. She had understood his action, and without a groan had accepted her fate. Indeed, she seemed incapable of any further speech or action. She was staring down at her husband's body, which she, for the first time, seemed fully to see. Was her look one of grief or of resentment for the part he had played so unintentionally in her child's death? It was hard to tell; and when, with slowly rising finger, she pointed to the pistol so tightly clutched in the other outstretched hand, no one there - and by this time the room was full - could foretell what her words would be when her tongue regained its usage and she could speak.

What she did say was this:

"Is there a bullet gone? Did he fire off that pistol?" A question so manifestly one of delirium that no one answered it, which seemed to surprise her, though she said nothing till her glance had passed all around the walls of the room to where a window stood open to the night – its lower sash being entirely raised. "There! Look there!" she cried, with a commanding accent, and, throwing up her hands, sank a dead weight into the arms of those supporting her.

No one understood; but naturally more than one rushed to the window. An open space was before them. Here lay the fields not yet parcelled out into lots and built upon; but it was not upon these they looked, but upon the strong trellis which they found there, which, if it supported no vine, formed a veritable ladder between this window and the ground.

Could she have meant to call attention to this fact; and were her words expressive of another idea than the obvious one of suicide?

If so, to what lengths a woman's imagination can go! Or so their combined looks seemed to proclaim, when to their utter astonishment they saw the officer, who had presented a calm appearance up till now, shift his position and with a surprised grunt direct their eyes to a portion of the wall just visible beyond the half-drawn curtains of the bed. The mirror hanging there showed a star-shaped breakage, such as follows the sharp impact of a bullet or a fiercely projected stone.

"He fired two shots. One went wild; the other straight home."

It was the officer delivering his opinion.

Mr Saunders, returning from the distant room where he had assisted in carrying Mrs Hammond, cast a look at the shattered glass, and remarked forcibly:

"I heard but one; and I was sitting up, disturbed by that poor infant. Jennie, did you hear more than one shot?" he asked, turning toward his wife.

"No," she answered, but not with the readiness he had evidently expected. "I heard only one, but that was not quite usual in its tone. I'm used to guns," she explained, turning to the officer. "My father was an army man, and he taught me very early to load and fire a pistol. There was a prolonged sound to this shot; something like an echo of itself, following close upon the first ping. Didn't you notice that, Warren?"

"I remember something of the kind," her husband allowed.

"He shot twice and quickly," interposed the policeman sententiously. "We shall find a spent bullet back of that mirror."

But when, upon the arrival of the coroner, an investigation was made of the mirror and the wall behind, no bullet was found either there or anywhere else in the room, save in the dead man's breast. Nor had more than one been shot from his pistol, as five full chambers testified. The case which seemed so simple had its mysteries, but the assertion made by Mrs Saunders no longer carried weight, nor was the evidence offered by the broken mirror considered as indubitably establishing the fact that a second shot had been fired in the room.

Yet it was equally evident that the charge which had entered the dead speculator's breast had not been delivered at the close range of the pistol found clutched in his hand. There were no powder-marks to be discerned on his pajama-jacket, or on the flesh beneath. Thus anomaly confronted anomaly, leaving open but one other theory: that the bullet found in Mr Hammond's breast came from the window and the one he shot went out of it. But this would necessitate his having shot his pistol from a point far removed from where he was found; and his wound was such as made it difficult to believe that he would stagger far, if at all, after its infliction.

Yet, because the coroner was both conscientious and alert, he caused a most rigorous search to be made of the ground overlooked by the above-mentioned window; a search in which the police joined, but which was without any result save that of rousing the attention of people in the neighbourhood and leading to a story being circulated of a man seen sometime the night before crossing the fields in a great hurry. But as no further particulars were forthcoming, and not even a description of the man to be had, no emphasis would have been laid upon this story had it not transpired that the moment a report of it had come to Mrs Hammond's ears (why is there always someone to carry these reports?) she roused from the torpor into which she had fallen, and in wild fashion exclaimed:

"I knew it! I expected it! He was shot through the window and by that wretch. He never shot himself." Violent declarations which trailed off into the one continuous wail, "O, my baby! my poor baby!"

Such words, even though the fruit of delirium, merited some sort of attention, or so this good coroner thought, and as soon as opportunity offered and she was sufficiently sane and quiet to respond to his questions, he asked her whom she had meant by that wretch, and what reason she had, or thought she had, of attributing her husband's death to any other agency than his own disgust with life.

And then it was that his sympathies, although greatly roused in her favour, began to wane. She met the question with a cold stare followed by a few ambiguous words out of which he could make nothing. Had she said *wretch*? She did not remember. They must not be influenced by anything she might have uttered in her first grief. She was well-nigh insane at the time. But of one thing they might be sure: her husband had not shot himself; he was too much afraid of death for such an act. Besides, he was too happy: Whatever folks might say, he was too fond of his family to wish to leave it.

Nor did the coroner or any other official succeed in eliciting anything further from her. Even when she was asked, with cruel insistence, how she explained the fact that the baby was found lying on the floor instead of in its crib, her only answer was: "His father was trying to soothe it. The child was crying dreadfully, as you have heard from those who were kept awake by him that night, and my husband was carrying him about when the shot came which caused George to fall and overlay the baby in his struggles."

"Carrying a baby about with a loaded pistol in his hand?" came back in stern retort.

She had no answer for this. She admitted when informed that the bullet extracted from her husband's body had been found to correspond exactly with those remaining in the five chambers of the pistol taken from his hand, that he was not only the owner of this pistol but was in the habit of sleeping with it under his pillow; but, beyond that, nothing: and this reticence, as well as her manner which was cold and repellent, told against her.

A verdict of suicide was rendered by the coroner's jury, and the life-insurance company, in which Mr Hammond had but lately insured himself for a large sum, taking advantage of the suicide clause embodied in the policy, announced its determination of not paying the same.

Such was the situation, as known to Violet Strange and the general public, on the day she was asked to see Mrs Hammond and learn what might alter her opinion as to the justice of this verdict and the stand taken by the Shuler Life Insurance Company.

The clock on the mantel in Miss Strange's rose-coloured boudoir had struck three, and Violet was gazing in some impatience at the door, when there came a gentle knock upon it, and the maid (one of the elderly, not youthful, kind) ushered in her expected visitor.

"You are Mrs Hammond?" she asked, in natural awe of the too black figure outlined so sharply against the deep pink of the seashell room.

The answer was a slow lifting of the veil which shadowed the features she knew only from the cuts she had seen in newspapers.

"You are – Miss Strange?" stammered her visitor; "the young lady who –

"I am," chimed in a voice as ringing as it was sweet. "I am the person you have come here to see. And this is my home. But that does not make me less interested in the unhappy, or less desirous of serving them. Certainly you have met with the two greatest losses which can come to a woman - I know your story well enough to say that - but what have you to tell me in proof that you should not lose your anticipated income as well? Something vital, I hope, else I cannot help you; something which you should have told the coroner's jury - and did not."

The flush which was the sole answer these words called forth did not take from the refinement of the young widow's expression, but rather added to it; Violet watched it in its ebb and flow and, seriously affected by it (why, she did not know, for Mrs Hammond had made no other appeal either by look or gesture), pushed forward a chair and begged her visitor to be seated.

"We can converse in perfect safety here," she said. "When you feel quite equal to it, let me hear what you have to communicate. It will never go any further. I could not do the work I do if I felt it necessary to have a confidant."

"But you are so young and so - so -"

"So inexperienced you would say and so evidently a member of what New Yorkers call 'society'. Do not let that trouble you. My inexperience is not likely to last long and my social pleasures are more apt to add to my efficiency than to detract from it."

With this Violet's face broke into a smile. It was not the brilliant one so often seen upon her lips, but there was something in its quality which carried encouragement to the widow and led her to say with obvious eagerness:

"You know the facts?"

"I have read all the papers."

"I was not believed on the stand."

"It was your manner -"

"I could not help my manner. I was keeping something back, and, being unused to deceit, I could not act quite naturally."

"Why did you keep something back? When you saw the unfavourable impression made by your reticence, why did you not speak up and frankly tell your story?"

"Because I was ashamed. Because I thought it would hurt me more to speak than to keep silent. I do not think so now; but I did then – and so made my great mistake. You must remember not only the awful shock of my double loss, but the sense of guilt accompanying it; for my husband and I had quarrelled that night, quarrelled bitterly – that was why I had run away into another room and not because I was feeling ill and impatient of the baby's fretful cries."

"So people have thought." In saying this, Miss Strange was perhaps cruelly emphatic. "You wish to explain that quarrel? You think it will be doing any good to your cause to go into that matter with me now?"

"I cannot say; but I must first clear my conscience and then try to convince you that quarrel or no quarrel, *he* never took his own life. He was not that kind. He had an abnormal fear of death. I do not like to say it but he was a physical coward. I have seen him turn pale at the least hint of danger. He could no more have turned that muzzle upon his own breast than he could have turned it upon his baby. Some other hand shot him, Miss Strange. Remember the open window, the shattered mirror; and *I think I know that hand.*"

Her head had fallen forward on her breast. The emotion she showed was not so eloquent of grief as of deep personal shame.

"You think you know the *man?*" In saying this, Violet's voice sank to a whisper. It was an accusation of murder she had just heard.

"To my great distress, yes. When Mr Hammond and I were married," the widow now proceeded in a more determined tone, "there was another man - a very violent one - who vowed even at the church door that George and I should never live out two full years together. We have not. Our second anniversary would have been in November."

"But - "

"Let me say this: the quarrel of which I speak was not serious enough to occasion any such act of despair on his part. A man would be mad to end his life on account of so slight a disagreement. It was not even on account of the person of whom I've just spoken, though that person had been mentioned between us earlier in the evening, Mr Hammond having come across him face to face that very afternoon in the subway. Up to this time neither of us had seen or heard of him since our wedding-day."

"And you think this person whom you barely mentioned, so mindful of his old grudge that he sought out your domicile, and with the intention of murder, climbed the trellis leading to your room and turned his pistol upon the shadowy figure which was all he could see in the semi-obscurity of a much lowered gas-jet?"

"A man in the dark does not need a bright light to see his enemy when he is intent upon revenge."

Miss Strange altered her tone.

"And your husband? You must acknowledge that he shot off his pistol whether the other did or not."

"It was in self-defence. He would shoot to save his own life - or the baby's."

"Then he must have heard or seen –"

"A man at the window."

"And would have shot there?"

"Or tried to."

"Tried to?"

"Yes; the other shot first – oh, I've thought it all out – causing my husband's bullet to go wild. It was his which broke the mirror."

Violet's eyes, bright as stars, suddenly narrowed.

"And what happened then?" she asked. "Why cannot they find the bullet?"

"Because it went out of the window; - glanced off and went out of the window." Mrs Hammond's tone was triumphant; her look spirited and intense.

Violet eyed her compassionately.

"Would a bullet glancing off from a mirror, however hung, be apt to reach a window so far on the opposite side?"

"I don't know; I only know that it did," was the contradictory, almost absurd, reply.

"What *was* the cause of the quarrel you speak of between your husband and yourself? You see, I must know the exact truth and all the truth to be of any assistance to you."

"It was - it was about the care I gave, or didn't give, the baby. I feel awfully to have to say it, but George did not think I did my full duty by the child. He said there was no need of its crying so; that if I gave it the proper attention it would not keep the neighbours and himself awake half the night. And I – I got angry and insisted that I did the best I could; that the child was naturally fretful and that if he wasn't satisfied with my way of looking after it, he might try his. All of which was very wrong and unreasonable on my part, as witness the awful punishment which followed.

"And what made you get up and leave him?"

"The growl he gave me in reply. When I heard that, I bounded out of bed and said I was going to the spare room to sleep; and if the baby cried he might just try what he could do himself to stop it."

"And he answered?"

"This, just this - I shall never forget his words as long as I live - 'If you go, you need not expect me to let you in again no matter what happens.' "

"He said that?"

"And locked the door after me. You see I could not tell all that."

"It might have been better if you had. It was such a natural quarrel and so unprovocative of actual tragedy."

Mrs Hammond was silent. It was not difficult to see that she had no very keen regrets for her husband personally But then he was not a very estimable man nor in any respect her equal.

"You were not happy with him," Violet ventured to remark.

"I was not a fully contented woman. But for all that he had no cause to complain of me except for the reason I have mentioned. I was not a very intelligent mother. But if the baby were living now - O, if he were living now - with what devotion I should care for him."

She was on her feet, her arms were raised, her face impassioned with feeling. Violet, gazing at her, heaved a little sigh. It was perhaps in keeping with the situation, perhaps extraneous to it, but whatever its source, it marked a change in her manner. With no further check upon her sympathy, she said very softly: "It is well with the child."

The mother stiffened, swayed, and then burst into wild weeping.

"But not with me," she cried, "not with me. I am desolate and bereft. I have not even a home in which to hide my grief and no prospect of one."

"But," interposed Violet, "surely your husband left you something? You cannot be quite penniless?"

"My husband left nothing," was the answer, uttered without bitterness, but with all the hardness of fact. "He had debts. I shall pay those debts. When these and other necessary expenses are liquidated, there will be but little left. He made no secret of the fact that he lived close up to his means. That is why he was induced to take on a life insurance. Not a friend of his but knows his improvidence. I - I have not even jewels. I have only my

---

determination and an absolute conviction as to the real nature of my husband's death."

"What is the name of the man you secretly believe to have shot your husband from the trellis?"

Mrs Hammond told her.

It was a new one to Violet. She said so and then asked:

"What else can you tell me about him?"

"Nothing, but that he is a very dark man and has a club-foot."

"Oh, what a mistake you've made."

"Mistake? Yes, I acknowledge that."

"I mean in not giving this last bit of information at once to the police. A man can be identified by such a defect. Even his footsteps can be traced. He might have been found that very day. Now, what have we to go upon?"

"You are right, but not expecting to have any difficulty about the insurance money I thought it would be generous in me to keep still. Besides, this is only surmise on my part. I feel certain that my husband was shot by another hand than his own, but I know of no way of proving it. Do you?"

Then Violet talked seriously with her, explaining how their only hope lay in the discovery of a second bullet in the room which had already been ransacked for this very purpose and without the shadow of a result.

A tea, a musicale, and an evening dance kept Violet Strange in a whirl for the remainder of the day. No brighter eye nor more contagious wit lent brilliance to these occasions, but with the passing of the midnight hour no one who had seen her in the blaze of electric lights would have recognised this favoured child of fortune in the earnest figure sitting in the obscurity of an uptown apartment, studying the walls, the ceilings, and the floors by the dim light of a lowered gas-jet. Violet Strange in society was a very different person from Violet Strange under the tension of her secret and peculiar work.

She had told them at home that she was going to spend the night with a friend; but only her old coachman knew who that friend was. Therefore a very natural sense of guilt mingled with her emotions at finding herself alone on a scene whose gruesome mystery she could solve only by identifying herself with the place and the man who had perished there.

Dismissing from her mind all thought of self, she strove to think as he thought, and act as he acted on the night when he found himself (a man of but little courage) left in this room with an ailing child.

At odds with himself, his wife, and possibly with the child screaming away in its crib, what would he be apt to do in his present emergency? Nothing at first, but as the screaming continued he would remember the old tales of fathers walking the floor at night with crying babies, and hasten to follow suit. Violet, in her anxiety to reach his inmost thought, crossed to where the crib had stood, and, taking that as a start, began pacing the room in search of the spot from which a bullet, if shot, would glance aside from the mirror in the direction of the window. (Not that she was ready to accept this theory of Mrs Hammond, but that she did not wish to entirely dismiss it without putting it to the test.)

She found it in an unexpected quarter of the room and much nearer the bed-head than where his body was found. This, which might seem to confuse matters, served, on the contrary, to remove from the case one of its most serious difficulties. Standing here, he was within reach of the pillow under which his pistol lay hidden, and if startled, as his wife believed him to have been by a noise at the other end of the room, had but to crouch and reach behind him in order to find himself armed and ready for a possible intruder.

Imitating his action in this as in other things, she had herself crouched low at the bedside and was on the point of withdrawing her hand from under the pillow, when a new surprise checked her movement and held her fixed in her position, with eyes staring straight at the adjoining wall. She had seen there what he must have seen in making this same turn – the dark bars of the opposite window-frame outlined in the mirror – and understood at once what had happened. In the nervousness and terror of the moment, George Hammond had mistaken this reflection of the window for the window itself, and shot impulsively at the man he undoubtedly saw covering him from the trellis without. But while this explained the shattering of the mirror, how about the other and still more vital question, of where the bullet went afterward? Was the angle at which it had been fired acute enough to send it out of a window diagonally opposed? No; even if the pistol had been held closer to the man firing it than she had reason to believe, the angle still would be oblique enough to carry it on to the further wall.

But no sign of any such impact had been discovered on this wall. Consequently, the force of the bullet had been expended before reaching it, and when it fell –

Here, her glance, slowly travelling along the floor, impetuously paused. It had reached the spot where the two bodies had been found, and unconsciously her eyes rested there, conjuring up the picture of the bleeding father and the strangled child. How piteous and how dreadful it all was. If she could only understand – Suddenly she rose straight up, staring and immovable in the dim light. Had the idea – the explanation-the only possible explanation covering the whole phenomena come to her at last?

It would seem so, for as she so stood, a look of conviction settled over her features, and with this look, evidences of a horror which for all her fast accumulating knowledge of life and its possibilities made her appear very small and very helpless.

A half-hour later, when Mrs Hammond, in her anxiety at hearing nothing more from Miss Strange, opened the door of her room, it was to find, lying on the edge of the sill, the little detective's card with these words hastily written across it:

I do not feel as well as I could wish, and so have telephoned to my own coachman to come and take me home. I will either see or write you within a few days. But do not allow yourself to hope. I pray you do not allow yourself the least hope; the outcome is still very problematical.

When Violet's employer entered his office the next morning it was to find a veiled figure awaiting him which he at once recognised as that of his little deputy. She was slow in lifting her veil and when it finally came free he felt a momentary doubt as to his wisdom in giving her just such a matter as this to investigate. He was quite sure of his mistake when he saw her face, it was so drawn and pitiful.

"You have failed," said he.

"Of that you must judge," she answered; and drawing near she whispered in his ear.

"No!" he cried in his amazement.

"Think," she murmured, "think. Only so can all the facts be accounted for."

"I will look into it; I will certainly look into it," was his earnest reply. "If you are right – But never mind that. Go home and take a horseback ride in the Park. When I have news in regard to this I will let you know. Till then forget it all. Hear me, I charge you to forget everything but your balls and your parties."

And Violet obeyed him.

Some few days after this, the following statement appeared in all the papers:

> Owing to some remarkable work done by the firm of ··· & ···, the well-known private detective agency, the claim made by Mrs George Hammond against the Shuler Life Insurance Company is likely to be allowed without further litigation. As our readers will remember, the contestant has insisted from the first that the bullet causing her husband's death came from another pistol than the one found clutched in his own hand. But while reasons were not lacking to substantiate this assertion, the failure to discover more than the disputed track of a second bullet led to a verdict of suicide, and a refusal of the company to pay.
>
> But now that bullet has been found. And where? In the most startling place in the world, viz: in the larynx of the child found lying dead upon the floor beside his father, strangled as was supposed by the weight of that father's arm. The theory is, and there seems to be none other, that the father, hearing a suspicious noise at the window, set down the child he was endeavouring to soothe and made for the bed and his own pistol, and, mistaking a reflection of the assassin for the assassin himself, sent his shot sidewise at a mirror just as the other let go the trigger which drove a similar bullet into his breast. The course of the one was straight and fatal and that of the other deflected. Striking the mirror at an oblique angle, the bullet fell to the floor where it was picked up by the crawling child, and, as was most natural, thrust at once into his mouth. Perhaps it felt hot to the little tongue; perhaps the child was simply frightened by some convulsive movement of the father who evidently spent his last moment in an endeavour to reach the child, but, whatever the cause, in the quick gasp it gave, the bullet was drawn into the larynx, strangling him.
>
> That the father's arm, in his last struggle, should have fallen directly across the little throat is one of those anomalies which confounds reason and misleads justice by stopping investigation at the very point where truth lies and mystery disappears.
>
> Mrs Hammond is to be congratulated that there are detectives who do not give too much credence to outward appearances.
>
> We expect soon to hear of the capture of the man who sped home the death-dealing bullet.

A Retrieved Reformation

'O. Henry'
(William Sydney Porter)

A guard came to the prison shoe-shop, where Jimmy Valentine was assiduously stitching uppers, and escorted him to the front office. There the warden handed Jimmy his pardon which had been signed that morning by the governor. Jimmy took it in a tired kind of way. He had served nearly ten months of a four-year sentence. He had expected to stay only about three months, at the longest. When a man with as many friends on the outside as Jimmy Valentine had is received in the 'stir' it is hardly worth while to cut his hair.

"Now, Valentine," said the warden, "you'll go out in the morning. Brace up, and make a man of yourself. You're not a bad fellow at heart. Stop cracking safes, and live straight."

"Me?" said Jimmy, in surprise. "Why, I never cracked a safe in my life."

"Oh, no," laughed the warden. "Of course not. Let's see, now. How was it you happened to get sent up on that Springfield job? Was it because you wouldn't prove an alibi for fear of

---

compromising somebody in extremely high-toned society? Or was it simply a case of a mean old jury that had it in for you? It's always one or the other with you innocent victims."

"Me?" said Jimmy, still blankly virtuous. "Why, warden, I never was in Springfield in my life!"

"Take him back, Cronin," smiled the warden, "and fix him up with outgoing clothes. Unlock him at seven in the morning, and let him come to the bull pen. Better think over my advice, Valentine."

At a quarter past seven on the next morning Jimmy stood in the warden's outer office. He had on a suit of the villainously fitting, ready-made clothes and a pair of the stiff, squeaky shoes that the state furnishes to its discharged compulsory guests.

The clerk handed him a railroad ticket and the five-dollar bill with which the law expected him to rehabilitate himself into good citizenship and prosperity. The warden gave him a cigar and shook hands. Valentine, 9762, was chronicled on the books 'Pardoned by Governor', and Mr James Valentine walked out into the sunshine.

Disregarding the song of the birds, the waving green trees and the smell of the flowers, Jimmy headed straight for a restaurant. There he tasted the first sweet joys of liberty in the shape of a broiled chicken and a bottle of white wine – followed by a cigar a grade better than the one the warden had given him. From there he proceeded leisurely to the depot. He tossed a quarter into the hat of a blind man sitting by the door, and boarded his train. Three hours set him down in a little town near the state line. He went to the cafe of one Mike Dolan and shook hands with Mike, who was alone behind the bar.

"Sorry we couldn't make it sooner, Jimmy, me boy," said Mike. "But we had that protest from Springfield to buck against, and the governor nearly balked. Feeling all right?"

"Fine," said Jimmy. "Got my key?"

He got his key and went upstairs, unlocking the door of a room at the rear. Everything was just as he had left it. There on the floor was still Ben Price's collar-button that had been torn from that eminent detective's shirt-band when they had overpowered Jimmy to arrest him.

Pulling out from the wall a folding-bed, Jimmy slid back a panel in the wall and dragged out a dust-covered suitcase. He opened this and gazed fondly at the finest set of burglar's tools in the East. It was a complete set, made of specially tempered steel, the latest designs in drills, punches, braces and bits, jimmies, clamps and augers, with two or three novelties invented by Jimmy himself, in which he took pride. Over nine hundred dollars they had cost him to have made at – a place where they make such things for the profession.

In half an hour Jimmy went downstairs and through the cafe. He was now dressed in tasteful and well-fitting clothes, and carried his dusted and cleaned suitcase in his hand.

"Got anything on?" asked Mike Dolan, genially.

"Me?" said Jimmy, in a puzzled tone. "I don't understand. I'm representing the New York Amalgamated Short Snap Biscuit Cracker and Frazzled Wheat Company."

This statement delighted Mike to such an extent that Jimmy had to take a seltzer-and-milk on the spot. He never touched 'hard' drinks.

A week after the release of Valentine, 9762, there was a neat job of safe burglary done in Richmond, Indiana, with no clue to the author. A scant eight hundred dollars was all that was secured. Two weeks after that a patented, improved, burglar-proof safe in Logansport was opened like a cheese to the tune of fifteen hundred dollars, currency; securities and silver untouched. That began to interest the rogue-catchers. Then an old-fashioned bank-safe in Jefferson City became active and threw out of its crater an eruption of bank-notes amounting to five thousand dollars. The losses were now high enough to bring the matter up into Ben Price's class of work. By comparing notes, a remarkable similarity in the methods of the burglaries was noticed. Ben Price investigated the scenes of the robberies and was heard to remark:

"That's Dandy Jim Valentine's autograph. He's resumed business. Look at that combination knob – jerked out as easy as pulling up a radish in wet weather. He's got the only clamps that can do it. And look how clean those tumblers were punched out! Jimmy never has to drill but one hole. Yes, I guess I want Mr. Valentine. He'll do his bit next time without any short-time or clemency foolishness."

Ben Price knew Jimmy's habits. He had learned them while working up the Springfield case. Long jumps, quick getaways, no confederates, and a taste for good society – these ways had helped Mr Valentine to become noted as a successful dodger of retribution. It was given out that Ben Price had taken up the trail of the elusive cracksman, and other people with burglarproof safes felt more at ease.

One afternoon Jimmy Valentine and his suitcase climbed out of the mail-hack in Elmore, a little town five miles off the railroad down in the blackjack country of Arkansas. Jimmy, looking like an athletic young senior just home from college, went down the board sidewalk toward the hotel.

A young lady crossed the street, passed him at the corner and entered a door over which was the sign 'The Elmore Bank'. Jimmy Valentine looked into her eyes, forgot what he was, and became another man. She lowered her eyes and coloured slightly. Young men of Jimmy's style and looks were scarce in Elmore.

Jimmy collared a boy that was loafing on the steps of the bank as if he were one of the stockholders, and began to ask him questions about the town, feeding him dimes at intervals. By and by the young lady came out, looking royally unconscious of the young man with the suitcase, and went her way.

"Isn't that young lady Miss Polly Simpson?" asked Jimmy, with specious guile.

"Naw," said the boy. "She's Annabel Adams. Her pa owns this bank. What'd you come to Elmore for? Is that a gold watch-chain? I'm going to get a bulldog. Got any more dimes?"

Jimmy went to the Planters' Hotel, registered as Ralph D. Spencer, and engaged a room. He leaned on the desk and declared his platform to the clerk. He said he had come to Elmore to look for a location to go into business. How was the shoe business, now, in the town? He had thought of the shoe business. Was there an opening?

The clerk was impressed by the clothes and manner of Jimmy. He, himself, was something of a pattern of fashion to the thinly gilded youth of Elmore, but he now perceived his shortcomings. While trying to figure out Jimmy's manner of tying his four-in-hand, he cordially gave information.

Yes, there ought to be a good opening in the shoe line. There wasn't an exclusive shoe-store in the place. The dry-goods and general stores handled them. Business in all lines was fairly good. Hoped Mr Spencer would decide to locate in Elmore. He would find it a pleasant town to live in, and the people very sociable.

Mr Spencer thought he would stop over in the town a few days and look over the situation. No, the clerk needn't call the boy. He would carry up his suitcase, himself; it was rather heavy.

Mr Ralph Spencer, the phoenix that arose from Jimmy Valentine's ashes – ashes left by the flame of a sudden and alternative attack of love – remained in Elmore, and prospered. He opened a shoe-store and secured a good run of trade.

Socially he was also a success, and made many friends. And he accomplished the wish of his heart. He met Miss Annabel Adams, and became more and more captivated by her charms.

At the end of a year the situation of Mr Ralph Spencer was this: he had won the respect of the community, his shoe-store was flourishing, and he and Annabel were engaged to be married in two weeks. Mr. Adams, the typical, plodding, country banker, approved of Spencer. Annael's pride in him almost equalled her affection. He was as much at home in the family of Mr Adams and that of Annabel's married sister as if he were already a member.

One day Jimmy sat down in his room and wrote this letter, which he mailed to the safe address of one of his old friends in St Louis:

Dear Old Pal:
I want you to be at Sullivan's place, in Little Rock, next Wednesday night at nine o'clock. I want you to wind up some little matters for me. And, also, I want to make you a present of my kit of tools. I know you'll be glad to get them - you couldn't duplicate the lot for a thousand dollars. Say, Billy, I've quit the old business - a year ago. I've got a nice store. I'm making an honest living, and I'm going to marry the finest girl on earth two weeks from now. It's the only life, Billy - the straight one. I wouldn't touch a dollar of another man's money now for a million. After I get married I'm going to sell out and go West, where there won't be so much danger of having old scores brought up against me. I tell you, Billy, she's an angel. She believes in me; and I wouldn't do another crooked thing for the whole world. Be sure to be at Sully's, for I must see you. I'll bring along the tools with me.
Your old friend,
Jimmy

On the Monday night after Jimmy wrote this letter, Ben Price jogged unobtrusively into Elmore in a livery buggy. He lounged about town in his quiet way until he found out what he wanted to know. From the drug-store across the street from Spencer's shoe-store he got a good look at Ralph D. Spencer.

"Going to marry the banker's daughter are you, Jimmy?" said Ben to himself, softly. "Well, I don't know!"

The next morning Jimmy took breakfast at the Adamses. He was going to Little Rock that day to order his wedding-suit and buy something nice for Annabel. That would be the first time he had left town since he came to Elmore. It had been more than a year now since those last professional 'jobs', and he thought he could safely venture out.

After breakfast quite a family party went downtown together – Mr. Adams, Annabel, Jimmy and Annabel's married sister with her two little girls, aged five and nine. They came by the hotel where Jimmy still boarded, and he ran up to his room and brought along his suitcase. Then they went on to the bank. There stood Jimmy's horse and buggy and Dolph Gibson, who was going to drive him over to the railroad station.

All went inside the high, carved oak railings into the banking-room – Jimmy included, for Mr Adams's future son-in-law was welcome anywhere. The clerks were pleased to be greeted by the good-looking, agreeable young man who was going to marry Miss Annabel. Jimmy set his suitcase down. Annabel, whose heart was bubbling with happiness and lively youth, put on Jimmy's hat and picked up the suitcase. "Wouldn't I make a nice drummer?" said Annabel. "My! Ralph, how heavy it is. Feels like it was full of gold bricks."

"Lot of nickel-plated shoehorns in there," said Jimmy, coolly, "that I'm going to return. Thought I'd save express charges by taking them up. I'm getting awfully economical."

The Elmore Bank had just put in a new safe and vault. Mr Adams was very proud of it, and insisted on an inspection by everyone. The vault was a small one, but it had a new patented door. It fastened with three solid steel bolts thrown simultaneously with a single handle, and had a time-lock. Mr. Adams beamingly explained its workings to Mr Spencer, who showed a courteous but

---

not too intelligent interest. The two children, May and Agatha, were delighted by the shining metal and funny clock and knobs.

While they were thus engaged Ben Price sauntered in and leaned on his elbow, looking casually inside between the railings. He told the teller that he didn't want anything; he was just waiting for a man he knew.

Suddenly there was a scream or two from the women, and a commotion. Unperceived by the elders, May, the nine-year-old girl, in a spirit of play, had shut Agatha in the vault. She had then shot the bolts and turned the knob of the combination as she had seen Mr Adams do.

The old banker sprang to the handle and tugged at it for a moment. "The door can't be opened," he groaned. "The clock hasn't been wound nor the combination set."

Agatha's mother screamed again, hysterically.

"Hush!" said Mr Adams, raising his trembling hand. "All be quiet for a moment. Agatha!" he called as loudly as he could. "Listen to me." During the following silence they could just hear the faint sound of the child wildly shrieking in the dark vault in a panic of terror.

"My precious darling!" wailed the mother. "She will die of fright! Open the door! Oh, break it open! Can't you men do something?"

"There isn't a man nearer than Little Rock who can open that door," said Mr Adams, in a shaky voice. "My God! Spencer, what shall we do? That child – she can't stand it long in there. There isn't enough air, and, besides, she'll go into convulsions from fright."

Agatha's mother, frantic now, beat the door of the vault with her hands. Somebody wildly suggested dynamite. Annabel turned to Jimmy, her large eyes full of anguish, but not yet despairing. To a woman nothing seems quite impossible to the powers of the man she worships.

"Can't you do something, Ralph – *try*, won't you?"

He looked at her with a queer, soft smile on his lips and in his keen eyes.

"Annabel," he said, "give me that rose you are wearing, will you?"

Hardly believing that she heard him aright, she unpinned the bud from the bosom of her dress and placed it in his hand. Jimmy stuffed it into his vest-pocket, threw off his coat and pulled up his shirtsleeves. With that act Ralph D. Spencer passed away and Jimmy Valentine took his place.

"Get away from the door, all of you," he commanded, shortly.

He set his suitcase on the table, and opened it out flat. From that time on he seemed to be unconscious of the presence of anyone else. He laid out the shining, queer implements swiftly and orderly, whistling softly to himself as he always did when at work. In a deep silence and immovable, the others watched him as if under a spell.

In a minute Jimmy's pet drill was biting smoothly into the steel door. In ten minutes – breaking his own burglarious record – he threw back the bolts and opened the door.

Agatha, almost collapsed, but safe, was gathered into her mother's arms.

Jimmy Valentine put on his coat and walked outside the railings toward the front door. As he went he thought he heard a far-away voice that he once knew call "Ralph!" But he never hesitated.

At the door a big man stood somewhat in his way.

"Hello, Ben!" said Jimmy, still with his strange smile. "Got around at last, have you? Well, let's go. I don't know that it makes much difference, now."

And then Ben Price acted rather strangely.

"Guess you're mistaken, Mr Spencer," he said. "Don't believe I recognise you. Your buggy's waiting for you, ain't it?"

And Ben Price turned and strolled down the street.

A Birthday

Katherine Mansfield

Andreas Binzer woke slowly. He turned over on the narrow bed and stretched himself – yawned – opening his mouth as widely as possible and bringing his teeth together afterwards with a sharp 'click'. The sound of that click fascinated him; he repeated it quickly several times, with a snapping movement of the jaws. What teeth! he thought. Sound as a bell, every man jack of them. Never had one out, never had one stopped. That comes of no tomfoolery in eating, and a good, regular brushing night and morning. He raised himself on his left elbow and waved his right arm over the side of the bed to feel for the chair where he put his watch and chain overnight. No chair was there – of course, he'd forgotten, there wasn't a chair in this wretched spare room. Had to put the confounded thing under his pillow. "Half-past eight, Sunday, breakfast at nine – time for the bath" – his brain ticked to the watch. He sprang out of bed and went over to the window. The venetian blind was broken, hung fan-shaped over the upper pane . . . "That blind must be mended. I'll get the office boy to drop in and fix it on his way home tomorrow – he's a good hand at blinds. Give him twopence and he'll do it as well as a carpenter . . . Anna could do it herself if she was all right. So would I, for the matter of that, but I don't like to trust myself on rickety step-ladders." He looked up at the sky: it shone, strangely white, unflecked with cloud; he looked down at the row of garden strips and backyards. The fence of these gardens was built along the edge of a gully, spanned by an iron suspension bridge, and the people had a wretched habit of throwing their empty tins over the fence into the gully. Just like them, of course! Andreas started counting the tins, and decided, viciously, to write a letter to the papers about it and sign it – sign it in full.

The servant girl came out of their back door into the yard, carrying his boots. She threw one down on the ground, thrust her hand into the other, and stared at it, sucking in her cheeks. Suddenly she bent forward, spat on the toecap, and started polishing with a brush rooted out of her apron pocket ... "Slut of a girl! Heaven knows what infectious disease may be breeding now in that boot. Anna must get rid of that girl – even if she has to do without one for a bit – as soon as she's up and about again. The way she chucked one boot down and then spat upon the other! She didn't care whose boots she'd got hold of. *She* had no false notions of the respect due to the master of the house." He turned away from the window and switched his bath towel from the washstand rail, sick at heart. "I'm too sensitive for a man – that's what's the matter with me. Have been from the beginning, and will be to the end."

There was a gentle knock at the door and his mother came in. She closed the door after her and leant against it. Andreas noticed that her cap was crooked, and a long tail of hair hung over her shoulder. He went forward and kissed her.

"Good-morning, mother; how's Anna?"

The old woman spoke quickly, clasping and unclasping her hands.

"Andreas, please go to Doctor Erb as soon as you are dressed."

"Why," he said, "is she bad?"

Frau Binzer nodded, and Andreas, watching her, saw her face suddenly change; a fine network of wrinkles seemed to pull over it from under the skin surface.

"Sit down on the bed a moment," he said. "Been up all night?"

"Yes. No, I won't sit down. I must go back to her. Anna has been in pain all night. She wouldn't have you disturbed before because she said you looked so run down yesterday. You told her you had caught a cold and been very worried."

Straightway Andreas felt he was being accused.

"Well, she made me tell her, worried it out of me; you know the way she does."Again Frau Binzer nodded.

"Oh yes, I know. She says, is your cold better, and there's a warm under-vest for you in the left-hand corner of the big drawer."

Quite automatically Andreas cleared his throat twice.

"Yes," he answered. "Tell her my throat certainly feels looser. I suppose I'd better not disturb her?"

"No, and besides, *time*, Andreas."

"I'll be ready in five minutes."

They went into the passage. As Frau Binzer opened the door of the front bedroom, a long wail came from the room.

That shocked and terrified Andreas. He dashed into the bathroom, turned on both taps as far as they would go, cleaned his teeth and pared his nails while the water was running.

"Frightful business, frightful business," he heard himself whispering. "And I can't understand it. It isn't as though it were her first – it's her third. Old Shäfer told me, yesterday, his wife simply 'dropped' her fourth. Anna ought to have had a qualified nurse. Mother gives way to her. Mother spoils her. I wonder what she meant by saying I'd worried Anna yesterday. Nice remark to make to a husband at a time like this. Unstrung, I suppose – and my sensitiveness again."

When he went into the kitchen for his boots, the servant girl was bent over the stove, cooking breakfast. "Breathing into that, now, I suppose," thought Andreas, and was very short with the servant girl. She did not notice. She was full of terrified joy and importance in the goings on upstairs. She felt she was learning the secrets of life with every breath she drew. Had laid the table that morning saying, "Boy", as she put down the first dish, "Girl", as she placed the second – it had worked out with the saltspoon to "Boy". "For two pins I'd tell the master that, to comfort him, like," she decided. But the master gave her no opening.

"Put an extra cup and saucer on the table," he said; "the doctor may want some coffee."

"The doctor, sir?" The servant girl whipped a spoon out of a pan, and spilt two drops of grease on the stove. "Shall I fry something extra?" But the master had gone, slamming the door after him. He walked down the street – there was nobody about at all – dead and alive this place on a Sunday morning. As he crossed the suspension bridge a strong stench of fennel and decayed refuse streamed from the gully, and again Andreas began concocting a letter. He turned into the main road. The shutters were still up before the shops. Scraps of newspaper, hay and fruit skins strewed the pavement; the gutters were choked with the leavings of Saturday night. Two dogs sprawled in the middle of the road, scuffling and biting. Only the public-house at the corner was open; a young barman slopped water over the doorstep.

Fastidiously, his lips curling, Andreas picked his way through the water. "Extraordinary how I am noticing things this morning. It's partly the effect of Sunday. I loathe a Sunday when Anna's tied by the leg and the children are away. On Sunday a man has the right to expect his family. Everything here's filthy, the whole place might be down with the plague, and will be, too, if this street's not swept away. I'd like to have a hand on the government ropes." He braced his shoulders. "Now for this doctor."

"Doctor Erb is at breakfast," the maid informed him. She showed him into the waiting-room, a dark and musty place, with some ferns under a glass-case by the window. "He says he won't be a minute, please sir, and there is a paper on the table."

"Unhealthy hole," thought Binzer, walking over to the window and drumming his fingers on the glass fern-shade. "At breakfast, is he? That's the mistake I made: turning out early on an empty stomach."

A milk cart rattled down the street, the driver standing at the back, cracking a whip; he wore an immense geranium flower stuck in the lapel of his coat. Firm as a rock he stood, bending back a little in the swaying cart. Andreas craned his neck to watch him all the way down the road, even after he had gone, listening for the sharp sound of those rattling cans.

"H'm, not much wrong with him," he reflected. "Wouldn't mind a taste of that life myself. Up early, work all over by eleven o'clock, nothing to do but loaf about all day until milking time." Which he knew was an exaggeration, but he wanted to pity himself.

The maid opened the door and stood aside for Doctor Erb. Andreas wheeled round; the two men shook hands.

"Well, Binzer," said the doctor jovially, brushing some crumbs from a pearl-coloured waistcoat, "son and heir becoming importunate?"

Up went Binzer's spirits with a bound. Son and heir, by Jove! He was glad to have to deal with a man again. And a sane fellow this, who came across this sort of thing every day of the week.

"That's about the measure of it, Doctor," he answered, smiling and picking up his hat. "Mother dragged me out of bed this morning with imperative orders to bring you along."

"Gig will be round in a minute. Drive back with me, won't you? Extraordinary, sultry day; you're as red as a beetroot already."

Andreas affected to laugh. The doctor had one annoying habit – imagined he had the right to poke fun at everybody simply because he was a doctor. "The man's riddled with conceit, like all these professionals," Andreas decided.

"What sort of a night did Frau Binzer have?" asked the doctor. "Ah, here's the gig. Tell me on the way up. Sit as near the middle as you can, will you, Binzer? Your weight tilts it over a bit one side – that's the worst of you successful businessmen."

"Two stone heavier than I, if he's a pound," thought Andreas. "The man may be all right in his profession – but heaven preserve me."

"Off you go, my beauty." Doctor Erb flicked the little brown mare. "Did your wife get any sleep last night?"

"No; I don't think she did," answered Andreas shortly. "To tell you the truth, I'm not satisfied that she hasn't a nurse."

"Oh, your mother's worth a dozen nurses," cried the doctor, with immense gusto. "To tell you the truth, I'm not keen on nurses – too raw – raw as rump-steak. They wrestle for a baby as though they were wrestling with Death for the body of Patroclus . . . Ever seen that picture by an English artist. Leighton? Wonderful thing – full of sinew!"

"There he goes again," thought Andreas, "airing off his knowledge to make a fool of me."

"Now your mother – she's firm – she's capable. Does what she's told with a fund of sympathy. Look at these shops we're passing – they're festering sores. How on earth this government can tolerate –"

"They're not so bad – sound enough – only want a coat of paint."

The doctor whistled a little tune and flicked the mare again.

"Well, I hope the young shaver won't give his mother too much trouble," he said. "Here we are."

A skinny little boy, who had been sliding up and down the back seat of the gig, sprang out and held the horse's head. Andreas went straight into the dining-room and left the servant girl to take the doctor upstairs. He sat down, poured out some coffee and bit through half a roll before helping himself to fish. Then he noticed there was no hot plate for the fish – the whole house was at sixes and sevens. He rang the bell, but the servant girl came in with a tray holding a bowl of soup and a hot plate.

"I've been keeping them on the stove," she simpered.

"Ah, thanks, that's very kind of you." As he swallowed the soup his heart warmed to this fool of a girl.

"Oh, it's a good thing Doctor Erb has come," volunteered the servant girl, who was bursting for want of sympathy.

"H'm, h'm," said Andreas.

She waited a moment, expectantly, rolling her eyes, then in full loathing of menkind went back to the kitchen and vowed herself to sterility.

Andreas cleared the soup bowl, and cleared the fish. As he ate, the room slowly darkened. A faint wind sprang up and beat the tree branches against the window. The dining-room looked over the breakwater of the harbour, and the sea swung heavily in rolling waves. Wind crept round the house, moaning drearily.

"We're in for a storm. That means I'm boxed up here all day. Well, there's one blessing; it'll clear the air." He heard the servant girl rushing importantly round the house, slamming windows. Then he caught a glimpse of her in the garden, unpegging tea towels from the line across the lawn. She was a worker, there was no doubt about that. He took up a book and wheeled his armchair over to the window. But it was useless. Too dark to read; he didn't believe in straining his eyes, and gas at ten o'clock in the morning seemed absurd. So he slipped down in the chair, leaned his elbows on the padded arms and gave himself up, for once, to idle dreaming. "A boy? Yes, it was bound to be a boy this time . . ." "What's your family, Binzer?" "Oh, I've two girls and a boy!" A very nice little number. Of course he was the last man to have a favourite child, but a man needed a son. "I'm working up the business for my son! Binzer & Son! It would mean living very tight for the next ten years, cutting expenses as fine as possible; and then –"

A tremendous gust of wind sprang upon the house, seized it, shook it, dropped, only to grip the more tightly. The waves swelled up along the breakwater and were whipped with broken foam. Over the white sky flew tattered streamers of grey cloud.

Andreas felt quite relieved to hear Doctor Erb coming down the stairs; he got up and lit the gas.

"Mind if I smoke in here?" asked Doctor Erb, lighting a cigarette before Andreas had time to answer. "You don't smoke, do you? No time to indulge in pernicious little habits!"

"How is she now?" asked Andreas, loathing the man.

"Oh, well as can be expected, poor little soul. She begged me to come down and have a look at you. Said she knew you were worrying." With laughing eyes the doctor looked at the breakfast table. "Managed to peck a bit, I see, eh?"

"Hoo-wih!" shouted the wind, shaking the window sashes.

"Pity, this weather," said Doctor Erb.

"Yes, it gets on Anna's nerves, and it's just nerve she wants."

"Eh, what's that?" retorted the doctor. "Nerve! Man alive! She's got twice the nerve of you and me rolled into one. Nerve! She's nothing but nerve. A woman who works as she does about the house and has three children in four years thrown in with the dusting, so to speak!"

He pitched his half-smoked cigarette into the fireplace and frowned at the window.

"Now *he's* accusing me," thought Andreas. "That's the second time this morning – first mother and now this man taking advantage of my sensitiveness." He could not trust himself to speak, and rang the bell for the servant girl.

"Clear away the breakfast things," he ordered. "I can't have them messing about on the table till dinner!"

"Don't be hard on the girl," coaxed Doctor Erb. "She's got twice the work to do today."

At that Binzer's anger blazed out.

"I'll trouble you, Doctor, not to interfere between me and my servants!" And he felt a fool at the same moment for not saying 'servant'.

Doctor Erb was not perturbed. He shook his head, thrust his hands into his pockets, and began balancing himself on toe and heel.

"You're jagged by the weather," he said wryly, "nothing else. A great pity – this storm. You know climate has an immense effect upon birth. A fine day perks a woman – gives her heart for her business. Good weather is as necessary to a confinement as it is to a washing day. Not bad – that last remark of mine – for a professional fossil, eh?"

Andreas made no reply.

"Well, I'll be getting back to my patient. Why don't you take a walk and clear your head? That's the idea for you."

"No," he answered, "I won't do that; it's too rough."

He went back to his chair by the window. While the servant girl cleared away he pretended to read . . . then his dreams! It seemed years since he had had the time to himself to dream like that – he never had a breathing space. Saddled with work all day, and couldn't shake it off in the evening, like other men. Besides, Anna was interested – they talked of practically nothing else together. Excellent mother she'd make for a boy; she had a grip of things.

Church bells started ringing through the windy air, now sounding as though from very far away, then again as though all the churches in the town had been suddenly transplanted into their street. They stirred something in him, those bells, something vague and tender. Just about that time Anna would call him from the hall. "Andreas, come and have your coat brushed. I'm ready." Then off they would go, she hanging on his arm and looking up at him. She certainly was a little thing. He remembered once saying when they were engaged, "Just as high as my heart," and she had jumped onto a stool and pulled his head down, laughing. A kid in those days, younger than her children in nature, brighter, more 'go' and 'spirit' in her. The way she'd run down the road to meet him after business! And the way she laughed when they were looking for a house. By Jove! That laugh of hers! At the memory he grinned, then grew suddenly grave. Marriage certainly changed a woman far more than it did a man. Talk about sobering down. She had lost all her go in two months! Well, once this boy business was over she'd get stronger. He began to plan a little trip for them. He'd take her away and they'd loaf about together somewhere. After all, dash it, they were young still. She'd got into a groove; he'd have to force her out of it, that's all.

He got up and went into the drawing-room, carefully shut the door and took Anna's photograph from the top of the piano. She wore a white dress with a big bow of some soft stuff under the chin, and stood, a little stiffly, holding a sheaf of artificial poppies and corn in her hands. Delicate she looked even then; her masses of hair gave her that look. She seemed to droop under the heavy braids of it, and yet she was smiling. Andreas caught his breath sharply. She was his wife – that girl. Posh! It had only been taken four years ago. He held it close to him, bent forward and kissed it. Then rubbed the glass with the back of his hand. At that moment, fainter than he had heard it in the passage, more terrifying, Andreas heard again that wailing cry. The wind caught it up in mocking echo, blew it over the housetops, down the street, far away from him. He flung out his arms, "I'm so damnably helpless," he said, and then to the picture, "Perhaps it's not as bad as it sounds; perhaps it is just my sensitiveness." In the half light of the drawing-room the smile seemed to deepen in Anna's portrait, and to become secret, even cruel. "No," he reflected, "that smile is not at all her happiest expression – it was a mistake to let her have it taken smiling like that. She doesn't look like my wife – like the mother of my son." Yes, that was it, she did not look like the mother of a son who was going to be a partner in the firm. The picture got on his nerves; he held it in different lights, looked at it from a distance, sideways, spent, it seemed to Andreas afterwards, a whole lifetime trying to fit it in. The more he played with it the deeper grew his dislike of it. Thrice he carried it over to the fireplace and decided to chuck it behind the Japanese umbrella in the grate; then he thought it absurd to waste an expensive frame. There was no good in beating about the bush. Anna looked like a stranger –

abnormal, a freak – it might be a picture taken just before or after death.

Suddenly he realised that the wind had dropped, that the whole house was still, terribly still. Cold and pale, with a disgusting feeling that spiders were creeping up his spine and across his face, he stood in the centre of the drawing-room, hearing Doctor Erb's footsteps descending the stairs.

He saw Doctor Erb come into the room; the room seemed to change into a great glass bowl that spun round, and Doctor Erb seemed to swim through this glass bowl towards him, like a goldfish in a pearl-coloured waistcoat.

"My beloved wife has passed away!" He wanted to shout it out before the doctor spoke.

"Well, she's hooked a boy this time!" said Doctor Erb. Andreas staggered forward.

"Look out. Keep on your pins," said Doctor Erb, catching Binzer's arm and murmuring, as he felt it, "Flabby as butter."

A glow spread all over Andreas. He was exultant.

"Well, by God! Nobody can accuse *me* of not knowing what suffering is," he said.

Mrs Cart

Jack Cox

(One of three stories that won Jack Cox *The Sydney Morning Herald* Young Writer of the Year competition as a Year 10 student in 2000.)

When I was eight years old and my mother was just beginning to shrivel into fifty, we lived in a dead fishing town on the edge of the sea. Our house sat wedged in salt, boldly thrusting towards the tide. She despised it, but nevertheless spent most of her days planted in its kitchen with her friends; numerous sets of heavily ringed fingers clasping scorching cups of tea in the icy cold wind.

On winter afternoons, when the wind that whipped from the backs of the churning waves made it impossible to stand outside, I would lie on the floorboards of our living room and stare stupidly at the ceiling. If I was still enough, I could hear the steady hum of my mother's conversations in the kitchen. It was like this I would learn that our butcher never put money in the collection plate at church, developers were coming to build a ferry port and that our next door neighbour, Mrs Cart, was a raving bitch.

Mrs Cart was an old widow who spent all day on her front porch, buried amongst heavy shawls and reading 1980s issues of *Women's Weekly*. I had no idea what a bitch was but, rather than confess my ignorance to my all-knowing mother, I let the word rattle noisily around in the back of my head until some days later, when I was walking past Mrs Cart's porch with money for a newspaper. I stopped and turned to face her scaly chin with a broad smile. I said good morning as politely as I could and told her that she looked like quite a bitch today. Then I turned and strolled slowly down the street, proud of my vocabulary extension.

I was not sent out for a newspaper for three weeks after that. Banished to the kitchen to make cups of tea for my mother and her friends, I was made to agree to never repeat the word again. When I asked what it meant, her foundation cracked under her cold glare and she claimed that if I was never going to repeat it, I had no use for a definition.

The house on the northern side of ours was a weathered old timber cottage with salt-streaked walls that had never felt the sting of paint. It was a bare place where Doug Marshal beat his wife until he passed out. Often I would lie awake in bed listening to the screams and slurred shouting that pounded against my window well into the night. My mother never spoke a word about it and, when Mr and Mrs Marshal said goodbye to each other at the gate in the morning, they kissed passionately, her naked leg sliding from her dressing gown and dragging in Doug's thigh. I would stare, fascinated, over my sodden cereal and through the window, with milk slipping from the corners of my absent mouth, until my mother slapped me gently across the head and told me to mind myself.

Every weekend Doug Marshal would drink until he was bloated and then drag himself through his front door, whisky staining the scattered stubble on his chin. Through the thin walls I could hear his soggy voice and the sound of her body against the furniture. Once a month he would burst into tears and run limply back out into the street. He would dash for the pier at the end of our street and stand, slanting over the water, crying out to the dark fish that sliced through the murk. Hanging on the edge of the sea, he would turn and shout defiantly into the empty streets that he just had to take one step.

Once a month the people in my street hurried from their houses, dressing gowns behind their bare legs like loose sails, until a volunteer coaxed Doug back to his wife. Quietly wiping the blood from her mouth, she took him back to bed.

The next day the street buzzed with boasting heroes and Doug Marshal would start to drink steadily for another four weeks.

After I was released from house arrest, I was wandering past Mrs Cart's porch, when she called out and invited me inside. I was led through tiny rooms blooming with ornaments and bric-a-brac and dirty couches that had the stitching worn away at the base. The air reeked of floor cleaner and licorice. All around me, sad, brown photos hid behind intricate frames on dusty dressers. Stopping to look at the frozen people inside them, I felt stale air prickle the back of my neck and turned to catch a glimpse of Mrs Cart sighing, her mouth drooping and her eyes locked far away in a world of memories.

I heard someone once say that she was an almost-war widow. Her husband had been called on to serve in the war when she was pregnant. Determined to live out his baby's childhood, he smashed his leg with a sledgehammer and was taken off the list. One week later he was struggling across the road under crutches when a car came roaring around the corner. Broken leg locking him to the asphalt, he couldn't get out of the way and was killed. The baby was a miscarriage.

I decided to ask Mrs Cart what a bitch was. She laughed, her double chin wobbling, then shoved a paper napkin full of scones into my hand and told me to take them home. My mother smiled at them and placed them under a tea towel. She told me that Mrs Cart was such a nice lady.

The Judgement
of Paris

Leonard Merrick

In the summer of the memorable year – , but the date doesn't matter, Robichon and Quinquart both paid court to Mademoiselle Brouette. Mademoiselle Brouette was a captivating actress, Robichon and Quinquart were the most comic of comedians, and all three were members of the Théâtre Suprême.

Robichon was such an idol of the public's that they used to laugh before he uttered the first word of his role; and Quinquart was so vastly popular that his silence threw the audience into convulsions.

Professional rivalry apart, the two were good friends, although they were suitors for the same lady, and this was doubtless due to the fact that the lady favoured the robust Robichon no more than she favoured the skinny Quinquart. She flirted with them equally, she approved them equally – and at last, when each of them had plagued her beyond endurance, she promised in a pet that she would marry the one that was the better actor.

Tiens! Not a player on the stage, not a critic on the Press could quite make up his mind which the better actor was. Only Suzanne Brouette could have said anything so tantalising.

"But how shall we decide the point, Suzanne?" stammered Robichon helplessly. "Whose pronouncement will you accept?"

"How can the question be settled?" queried Quinquart, dismayed. "Who shall be the judge?"

"Paris shall be the judge," affirmed Suzanne. "We are the servants of the public – I will take the public's word!"

Of course she was as pretty as a picture, or she couldn't have done these things.

Then poor Quinquart withdrew, plunged in reverie. So did Robichon. Quinquart reflected that she had been talking through her expensive hat. Robichon was of the same opinion. The public lauded them both, was no less generous to one than to the other – to wait for the judgement of Paris appeared equivalent to postponing the matter sine die. No way out presented itself to Quinquart. None occurred to Robichon.

"Mon vieux," said the latter, as they sat on the terrace of their favourite café a day or two before the annual vacation, "let us discuss this amicably. Have a cigarette! You are an actor, therefore you consider yourself more talented than I. I, too, am an actor, therefore I regard you as less gifted than myself. So much for our artistic standpoints! But we are also men of the world, and it must be obvious to both of us that we might go on being funny until we reached our deathbeds without demonstrating the supremacy of either. Enfin, our only hope lies in versatility – the conqueror must distinguish himself in a solemn part!" He viewed the other with complacence, for the quaint Quinquart had been designed for a droll by Nature.

"Right!" said Quinquart. He contemplated his colleague with satisfaction, for it was impossible to fancy the fat Robichon in tragedy.

"I perceive only one drawback to the plan," continued Robichon. "The Management will never consent to accord us a chance. Is it not always so in the theatre? One succeeds in a certain line of business and one must be resigned to play that line as long as one lives. If my earliest success had been scored as a villain of melodrama, it would be believed that I was competent to enact nothing but villains of melodrama; it happened that I made a hit as a comedian, wherefore nobody will credit that I am capable of anything but being comic."

"Same here!" concurred Quinquart. "Well, then, what do you propose?"

Robichon mused. "Since we shall not be allowed to do ourselves justice on the stage, we must find an opportunity off it!"

"A private performance? Good! Yet, if it is a private performance, how is Paris to be the judge?"

"Ah," murmured Robichon, "that is certainly a stumbling-block."

They sipped their apéritifs moodily. Many heads were turned towards the little table where they sat. "There are Quinquart and Robichon, how amusing they always are!" said passersby, little guessing the anxiety at the laughter-makers' hearts.

"What's to be done?" sighed Quinquart at last.

Robichon shrugged his fat shoulders, with a frown.

Both were too absorbed to notice that, after a glance of recognition, one of the pedestrians had paused, and was still regarding them irresolutely. He was a tall, burly man, habited in rusty black, and the next moment, as if finding courage, he stepped forward and spoke:

"Gentlemen, I ask pardon for the liberty I take – impulse urges me to seek your professional advice! I am in a position to pay a moderate fee. Will you permit me to explain myself?"

"Monsieur," returned Robichon, "we are in deep consideration of our latest parts. We shall be pleased to give you our attention at some other time."

"Alas!" persisted the newcomer, "with me time presses. I, too, am considering my latest part – and it will be the only speaking part I have ever played, though I have been 'appearing' for twenty years."

"What? You have been a super for twenty years?" said Quinquart, with a grimace.

"No, monsieur," replied the stranger grimly. "I have been the public executioner; and I am going to lecture on the horrors of the post I have resigned."

The two comedians stared at him aghast. Across the sunlit terrace seemed to have fallen the black shadow of the guillotine.

"I am Jacques Roux," the man went on. "I am 'trying it on the dog' at Appeville-sous-Bois next week, and I have what you gentlemen call 'stage fright' – I, who never knew what nervousness meant before! Is it not queer? As often as I rehearse walking on to the platform, I feel myself to be all arms and legs – I don't know what to do with them. Formerly, I scarcely remembered my arms and legs; but, of course, my attention used to be engaged by the other fellow's head. Well, it struck me that you might consent to give me a few hints in deportment. Probably one lesson would suffice."

"Sit down," said Robichon. "Why did you abandon your official position?"

"Because I awakened to the truth," Roux answered. "I no longer agree with capital punishment; it is a crime that should be abolished."

"The scruples of conscience, hein?"

"That is it."

"Fine!" said Robichon. "What dramatic lines such a lecture might contain! And of what is it to consist?"

"It is to consist of the history of my life – my youth, my poverty, my experiences as Executioner, and my remorse."

"Magnificent!" said Robichon. "The spectres of your victims pursue you even to the platform. Your voice fails you, your eyes start from your head in terror. You gasp for mercy, and imagination splashes your outstretched hands with gore. The audience thrill, women swoon, strong men are breathless with emotion." Suddenly he smote the table with his big fist, and little Quinquart nearly fell off his chair, for he divined the inspiration of his rival. "Listen!" cried Robichon, "are you known at Appeville-sous-Bois?"

"My name is known, yes."

"Bah! I mean are you known personally, have you acquaintances there?"

"Oh, no. But why?"

"There will be nobody to recognise you?"

"It is very unlikely in such a place."

"What do you estimate that your profits will amount to?"

"It is only a small hall, and the prices are cheap. Perhaps two hundred and fifty francs."

"And you are nervous, you would like to postpone your début?"

"I should not be sorry, I admit. But, again, why?"

"I will tell you why – I offer you five hundred francs to let me take your place!"

"Monsieur!"

"Is it a bargain?"

"I do not understand!"

"I have a whim to figure in a solemn part. You can explain next day that you missed your train – that you were ill, there are a dozen explanations that can be made; you will not be supposed to know that I personated you – the responsibility for that is mine. What do you say?"

"It is worth double the money," demurred the man.

"Not a bit of it! All the Press will shout the story of my practical joke – Paris will be astounded that I, Robichon, lectured as Jacques Roux and curdled an audience's blood. Millions will speak of your intended lecture tour who otherwise would never have heard of it. I am giving you the grandest advertisement, and paying you for it, besides. Enfin, I will throw a deportment lesson in! Is it agreed?"

"Agreed, monsieur!" said Roux.

Oh, the trepidation of Quinquart! Who could eclipse Robichon if his performance of the part equalled his conception of it? At the theatre that evening Quinquart followed Suzanne about the wings pathetically. He was garbed like a buffoon, but he felt like Romeo. The throng that applauded his capers were far from suspecting the romantic longings under his magenta wig. For the first time in his life he was thankful that the author hadn't given him more to do.

And, oh, the excitement of Robichon! He was to put his powers to a tremendous test, and if he made the effect that he anticipated he had no fear of Quinquart's going one better. Suzanne, to whom he whispered his project proudly, announced an intention of being present to 'see the fun'. Quinquart also promised to be there. Robichon sat up all night preparing his lecture.

If you wish to know whether Suzanne rejoiced at the prospect of his winning her, history is not definite on the point; but some chroniclers assert that at this period she made more than usual of Quinquart, who had developed a hump as big as the Pantheon.

And they all went to Appeville-sous-Bois.

Though no one in the town was likely to know the features of the Executioner, it was to be remembered that people there might know the actor's, and Robichon had made up to resemble Roux as closely as possible. Arriving at the humble hall, he was greeted by the lessee, heard that a 'good house' was expected, and smoked a cigarette in the retiring-room while the audience assembled.

At eight o'clock the lessee reappeared.

"All is ready, Monsieur Roux," he said.

Robichon rose.

He saw Suzanne and Quinquart in the third row, and was tempted to wink at them.

"Ladies and gentlemen –"

All eyes were riveted on him as he began; even the voice of the 'Executioner' exercised a morbid fascination over the crowd. The men nudged their neighbours appreciatively, and women gazed at him, half horrified, half charmed.

The opening of his address was quiet enough – there was even a humorous element in it, as he narrated imaginary experiences of his boyhood. People tittered, and then glanced at one another with an apologetic air, as if shocked at such a monster's daring to amuse them. Suzanne whispered to Quinquart: "Too cheerful; he hasn't struck the right note." Quinquart whispered back gloomily: "Wait; he may be playing for the contrast!"

And Quinquart's assumption was correct. Gradually the cheerfulness faded from the speaker's voice, the humorous incidents were past. Gruesome, hideous, grew the anecdotes. The hall shivered. Necks were craned, and white faces twitched suspensively. He dwelt on the agonies of the Condemned, he recited crimes in detail, he mirrored the last moments before the blade fell. He shrieked his remorse, his lacerating remorse. "I am a murderer," he sobbed; and in the hall one might have heard a pin drop.

There was no applause when he finished – that set the seal on his success; he bowed and withdrew amid tense silence. Still none moved in the hall, until, with a rush, the representatives of the Press sped forth to proclaim Jacques Roux an unparalleled sensation.

The triumph of Robichon! How generous were the congratulations of Quinquart, and how sweet the admiring tributes of Suzanne! And there was another compliment to come – nothing less than a card from the Marquis de Thevenin, requesting an interview at his home.

"Ah!" exclaimed Robichon, enravished, "an invitation from a noble! That proves the effect I made, hein?"

"Who may he be?" inquired Quinquart. "I never heard of the Marquis de Thevenin!"

"It is immaterial whether you have heard of him," replied Robichon. "He is a marquis, and he desires to converse with me! It is an honour that one must appreciate. I shall assuredly go."

And, being a bit of a snob, he sought a fiacre in high feather.

The drive was short, and when the cab stopped he was distinctly taken aback to perceive the unpretentious aspect of the nobleman's abode. It was, indeed, nothing better than a lodging. A peasant admitted him, and the room to which he was ushered boasted no warmer hospitality than a couple of candles and a decanter of wine. However, the sconces were massive silver. Monsieur le marquis, he was informed, had been suddenly compelled to summon his physician, and begged that Monsieur Roux would allow him a few minutes' grace.

Robichon ardently admired the candlesticks, but began to think he might have supped more cosily with Suzanne.

It was a long time before the door opened.

The Marquis de Thevenin was old – so old that he seemed to be falling to pieces as he tottered forward. His skin was yellow and shrivelled, his mouth sunken, his hair sparse and grey; and from this weird face peered strange eyes – the eyes of a fanatic.

"Monsieur, I owe you many apologies for my delay," he wheezed. "My unaccustomed exertion this evening fatigued me, and on my return from the hall I found it necessary to see my doctor. Your lecture was wonderful, Monsieur Roux – most interesting and instructive; I shall never forget it."

Robichon bowed his acknowledgments.

"Sit down, Monsieur Roux, do not stand! Let me offer you some wine. I am forbidden to touch it myself. I am a poor host, but my age must be my excuse."

"To be the guest of monsieur le marquis," murmured Robichon, "is a privilege, an honour, which – er –"

"Ah," sighed the Marquis. "I shall very soon be in the Republic where all men are really equals and the only masters are the worms. My reason for requesting you to come was to speak of your unfortunate experiences – of a certain unfortunate experience in particular. You referred in your lecture to the execution of one called Victor Lesueur. He died game, hein?"

"As plucky a soul as I ever dispatched!" said Robichon, savouring the burgundy.

"Ah! Not a tremor? He strode to the guillotine like a man?"

"Like a hero!" said Robichon, who knew nothing about him.

"That was fine," said the Marquis; "that was as it should be! You have never known a prisoner to die more bravely?" There was a note of pride in his voice that was unmistakable.

"I shall always recall his courage with respect," declared Robichon, mystified.

"Did you respect it at the time?"

"Pardon, Monsieur le Marquis?"

"I inquire if you respected it at the time; did you spare him all needless suffering?"

"There is no suffering," said Robichon. "So swift is the knife that –"

The host made a gesture of impatience. "I refer to mental suffering. Cannot you realise the emotions of an innocent man condemned to a shameful death?"

"Innocent! As for that, they all say that they are innocent."

"I do not doubt it. Victor, however, spoke the truth. I know it. He was my son."

"Your son?" faltered Robichon, aghast.

"My only son – the only soul I loved on earth. Yes; he was innocent, Monsieur Roux. And it was you who butchered him – he died by your hands."

"I – I was but the instrument of the law," stammered Robichon. "I was not responsible for his fate, myself."

"You have given a masterly lecture, Monsieur Roux," said the Marquis musingly; "I find myself in agreement with all that you said in it – 'you are his murderer'. I hope the wine is to your taste, Monsieur Roux? Do not spare it!"

"The wine?" gasped the actor. He started to his feet, trembling – he understood.

"It is poisoned," said the old man calmly. "In an hour you will be dead."

"Great Heavens!" moaned Robichon. Already he was conscious of a strange sensation – his blood was chilled, his limbs were weighted, there were shadows before his eyes.

"Ah, I have no fear of you!" continued the other; "I am feeble, I could not defend myself; but your violence would avail you nothing. Fight, or faint, as you please – you are doomed."

For some seconds they stared at each other dumbly – the actor paralysed by terror, the host wearing the smile of a lunatic. And then the 'lunatic' slowly peeled court-plaster from his teeth, and removed features, and lifted a wig.

And when the whole story was published, a delighted Paris awarded the palm to Quinquart without a dissentient voice, for while Robichon had duped an audience, Quinquart had duped Robichon himself.

Robichon bought the silver candlesticks, which had been hired for the occasion, and he presented them to Quinquart and Suzanne on their wedding-day.